Winner Books are produced by Victor Books and are designed to entertain and instruct young readers in Christian principles. Each book has been approved by specialists in Christian education and children's literature. These books uphold the teachings and principles of the Bible.

Other Winner Books you will enjoy:
Sarah and the Magic Twenty-fifth, by Margaret Epp
Sarah and the Pelican, by Margaret Epp
Sarah and the Lost Friendship, by Margaret Epp
Sarah and the Mystery of the Hidden Boy, by Margaret Epp
The Hairy Brown Angel and Other Animal Tails, edited by Grace Fox Anderson
The Peanut Butter Hamster and Other Animal Tails, edited by Grace Fox Anderson
Gopher Hole Treasure Hunt, by Ralph Bartholomew
Daddy, Come Home, by Irene Aiken
Battle at the Blue Line, by P.C. Fredricks
Patches, by Edith Buck
The Taming of Cheetah, by Lee Roddy
Ted and the Secret Club, by Bernard Palmer
The Mystery Man of Horseshoe Bend, by Linda Boorman

DANGER ON THE ALASKAN TRAIL
by H. W. Bailey

plus

The Mysterious Camel of India
by Grace Vernon

and the

Israeli Oil Well Mystery
by Bernard Palmer

A Winner Book

VICTOR BOOKS
a division of SP Publications, Inc.
WHEATON, ILLINOIS 60187

Offices also in Fullerton, California • Whitby, Ontario, Canada • Amersham-on-the-Hill, Bucks, England

Third printing, 1980

All Scripture quotations are from the King James Version.
Stories taken from *Counselor* with permission of
Scripture Press Publications.

Library of Congress Catalog Card No. 77–075906
ISBN: 0-88207-478-4

VICTOR BOOKS
A division of SP Publications, Inc.
P.O. Box 1825 . Wheaton, Ill. 60187

Contents

DANGER
ON THE
ALASKAN TRAIL

H. W. Bailey

Chapter 1

"I HATE to let you go alone, Son," Dr. Hugh Peterson said to Jim. "It's 200 miles to Fairbanks and it'll be a hard trip."

It was a cold February day in 1947. Their breath hung in clouds as father and son loaded the dogsled in front of their log house near Nolan, Alaska.

Young Jim straightened up and pushed his dark hair under his parka hood. "Dad, you've got to have that medicine, and the sick Eskimos here need you. Please don't worry about me."

"If only one man were well enough to go along . . ." his father began. "Our supply of medicine will last only about 12 more days if this epidemic keeps on. And without a shortwave transmitter and license, I can't even radio Fairbanks and have them fly the medicines in."

"Mountie and I will do our best," Jim said with a grin. He knelt beside the big silver-chested husky and hugged the dog.

In an hour the sled was packed. Jim went into the house to kiss his mother and younger sisters good-bye. He felt scared as he thought of the long trip ahead, but he said,

9

"Don't worry, Mom."

"Let's pray before you go," his dad suggested. The family stood in a circle, holding hands while Dr. Peterson prayed.

"Lord, we're sending our boy out on a dangerous trip. We hate to do it, but there seems to be no other way. We commit him into Your keeping now. We ask that You will give him a safe trip back with the medicine."

The tension in Jim's stomach eased up as his dad prayed. Of course the Lord would go with him and take care of him.

His mother had tears in her eyes as she watched him get behind the dogsled. His 11-year-old sister, Mary Beth, looked a little envious. She stood, holding baby Sarah in her arms just inside the door, waving.

The last thing his dad said to him still rang in his ears as the huskies started pulling: "Son, remember 'they that wait upon the Lord shall renew their strength: they shall mount up with wings as eagles; they shall run, and not be weary; and they shall walk, and not faint.'" [1]

Jim's missionary family had often experienced God's loving care when they had "waited" for Him to work. Jim knew God wouldn't fail them now.

"Mush! Mush!" Jim shouted to his waiting team. A sense of adventure surged through him as they put the little mission station far behind.

It was a fairly easy run along the Middle Fork River from Nolan to Coldfoot. The dogs were fresh and eager. The trail, for the most part, was downgrade. Occasionally, Jim rode the runners. But with the temperature near −40°,

---

[1] Isaiah 40:31

he kept warmer by running along behind the sled.

As he ran, Jim looked over his dogs with pride. They were all true huskies, and pulled smooth and steady. But to Jim, only one dog—Mountie—really mattered. He was a beauty. A born leader.

"He's a Mackenzie River husky," Dad had said the day he handed the squirming bundle of fur to Jim "Yes, a .Mackenzie River husky, with traces of Siberian and fox-hound in his ancestry. That should give him a great com-bination of endurance and speed."

Jim still remembered what his father had said though it was four years since Mountie had joined their family. And his father had been right!

When Jim had learned that Mountie had been bought from a Canadian Mounted Police officer, he had decided on the dog's name.

Now Mountie was Jim's best friend. He talked to the dog as he would to a friend since friends were few out in the Alaskan wilderness.

Only one thing troubled Jim. A dog such as Mountie would bring big money from anyone in Alaska. Jim shivered as he remembered the cruel-looking man named Aluk.

The man was suspected of stealing from the Eskimos' fur traps. Several times when he had met Jim and his dad out on the trail, he had boasted that he would own Mountie one day. Jim knew Aluk would stop at nothing to get the dog if he thought he could.

A mile out of Coldfoot Jim turned the team off the main trail and headed south toward Goldbench and Grubstake. He planned to stop at Grubstake for the night.

Jim slipped off his fur mittens and pulled back the

sleeve of his parka to look at his watch. It was 1 o'clock. It would get dark around 5 in the afternoon. "Let's see," he muttered, "Goldbench is about 20 miles. Grubstake is 10 miles farther. That's 30 altogether."

He pulled his mitten back on and spoke to the team. "We'll have to keep up a good pace, huskies, or it will be dark before we get to Grubstake. Mush! Mush!"

Something about the feel of the air warned Jim that bad weather was on the way. The dogs seemed to sense it too. As they sped along, Jim kept an eye on the sky. Gradually, it turned from bright blue to gray.

Tiny, swirling snowflakes began to fall—a few at first. But three hours later, as they were leaving Goldbench, the wind-driven snow stung his face.

With the growing storm, darkness would come quickly. Jim was thankful that Grubstake was not far ahead.

His thoughts were on food and rest, when suddenly he noticed Mountie sniffing the air as he raced along. Through the falling snow, Jim thought he saw the form of a man. He blinked hard and peered again.

Sure enough, it was a man, fur-clad, and carrying a gun. Jim recognized the fellow now, and a chill shot up his spine. Those squinting eyes, that sneering grin, the leather-like face belonged to only one man—Aluk.

Jim halted the team and moved quickly up to Mountie's side. The big dog was rigid, and the thick fur on his neck stood straight up. A low growl rumbled deep in his throat.

"Easy, boy," Jim spoke, as he laid his hand on Mountie's head. Quickly, and without taking his eyes off Aluk, Jim knelt and unfastened the dog's harness.

Seeing Jim's action, Aluk spoke. "So you give 'um Mountie me, no trouble. Ha, you one smart boy."

"Give Mountie to you?" Jim shouted back. "Do you think I'm crazy? Why, I wouldn't even sell him—not to you or anyone else—for any price!"

Jim was scared. More scared than he had ever been in his life. If only Aluk didn't have that gun! The wind wailed a lonely dirge across the snow and ice, and he shivered.

As Aluk's squinty eyes narrowed, Jim sent up a quick prayer for guidance. Aluk lifted his rifle and pointed it at Jim. "Give me dog or I shoot!" he threatened.

But Jim hardly heard him. Instead, he cocked his head to one side, trying to appear very interested in something just behind Aluk's back. And Aluk did just what Jim hoped he would.

Overcome with curiosity, the man glanced slowly back over his shoulder. That slow, uncertain move gave Jim the chance he had hoped for. He slapped Mountie's side sharply and whispered "go" into the dog's ear.

Like an arrow, the husky shot forward and landed with savage force on the surprised Aluk.

The man sprawled in the snow, dropping his gun. With a terrified cry, he threw up his arms to protect his throat from the angry dog. Jim grabbed the gun and yelled, "Hold it, Mountie!"

Slowly, the dog released his hold on Aluk. Jim realized then that Mountie would have ended the man's life in seconds. Never before had he seen his dog so fierce. But then Mountie had never before needed to protect his master's life in this manner.

Chapter 2

GINGERLY, ALUK picked himself up. Mountie circled him slowly, ready to attack again at the first word from his master. Aluk cursed as Jim threw the gun into a high mound of snow.

Sure now that Aluk could do them no harm, Jim called to the dog. Mountie came and stood at his side. But Jim had misjudged the craftiness of the man. Quickly, Aluk reached inside his fur parka and pulled out a 10-inch knife.

"You put'um Mountie to harness," he ordered. "Go with me. You not so smart as you think."

Jim broke out in a sweat. To send Mountie charging in now would be foolish. One plunge of that knife in the dog's throat would finish him.

"You hear me? Put Mountie to harness!" Aluk was impatient now.

Without replying, Jim hitched Mountie to the harness and stood back, watching Aluk come closer.

Mountie growled and crouched, ready to spring. "Easy there, Mountie. Everything will be all right," Jim spoke more hopefully than he felt.

"Yasss. You right. Everything be all right if you do what Aluk tell'um you."

"OK, Aluk," said Jim. "But can't we make some kind of bargain so I can go on? People's lives depend on my trip."

"Now you talk sense. Why you not say thees before? What you take for Mountie?"

"Oh, no. I didn't mean that." Jim paused, fighting against what he was going to say next, for he loved all his faithful dogs. "I meant—you—you can take any two of the other dogs instead . . ."

"Ho, Ho!" Aluk jeered. "You theenk Aluk crazee? No five dogs in world like Mountie."

"Sorry then," Jim answered. "Because you won't get Mountie—not alive."

"Him no good dead," sneered Aluk. "Besides you have trip to make, you say."

True, Jim realized. Getting the medicine back to his father was more important even than Mountie. It might mean saving hundreds of lives. And if his father could help the Eskimos now, they would be more open to receive the Gospel later.

"OK," Jim said, trying to keep his voice steady. "I guess I'll have to do what you say."

"Good. Now you talk sense. You go front of team. Me take driver place, tell'um you where to go," spat the leathery-faced Aluk.

Jim went up ahead with Mountie and Aluk took the driver's position behind the sled.

He looked back, and Aluk pointed out the direction they were to take. "You go that way," the man shouted.

Jim was thankful for two things: He was near Mountie

and Aluk had pointed straight toward Grubstake. At least they were moving in the direction Jim wanted to go.

"Mush . . . Mush . . . ," Aluk snarled. The dogs responded, but grudgingly. Jim knew if he hadn't been leading them, Aluk would have had plenty of trouble with the team.

As Jim plowed along, he was dismayed to see how dark it was getting. Where would they end up? Just then Aluk's harsh command interrupted his thoughts. Jim looked back.

"Go that way," Aluk pointed left now—off the trail to Grubstake. Jim's heart sank. Where were they going?

For some 20 minutes they continued on a straight course. Then Aluk cried, "Stop!"

It was dark now. The wind was whipping the snow around in blustery, blinding whirlpools. It it hadn't been for Aluk, Jim and the dogs would have been in Grubstake, comfortably settled for the night.

"Unhitch your dogs," Aluk snapped. "We go in here."

Jim could see no shelter, but this must be their stopping place for the night. Or would it be for longer? The thought angered him. He couldn't lose precious time now.

Still, he moved obediently down the line, unfastening the harness snaps. Mountie moved with him as he loosened each dog.

When the job was done, Aluk took Jim's arm in a crushing grip. "Come!" he barked as he forced his captive forward. Jim caught the glint of the steel blade in the man's hand.

Mountie followed, but the other dogs stayed outdoors.

Aluk and his captives had gone about 10 paces when Jim was able to make out the shape of a crude log building. It was so heavily covered with snow that it could have been mistaken for a mound of ice and snow.

Aluk shoved the door open. "Go in!" He gestured with a sweep of his arm.

Jim stumbled into the dark building, Mountie beside him. Aluk followed. He seemed to have no trouble finding his way around. In an instant, he thrust a kerosene lantern and some matches into Jim's hand. "You light lamp," he commanded.

Jim struck a match on the side of the lantern and held the flickering flame to the wick. The yellow light flared up, and he lowered the glass chimney.

Aluk pointed to a large wooden box. "Set the lamp there," he said.

As Jim moved to obey, he glanced quickly around the room. It was only one room really, but right across the back of it ran a partition of heavy wire fencing.

The wire ran from wall to wall and from floor to ceiling, forming a cage. Near one wall was a door in the wire partition. Except for its braces, the door was made of the same stout wire. On the door, he noticed, was a bright new combination lock.

Behind the wire, Jim could see a big animal, and for a moment, he felt sheer terror.

But as he stared, he realized he was wrong. It was a huge pile of fur pelts. So Aluk really *was* a thief. And this must be his hideout for the valuable furs!

Jim didn't have long to think. Aluk fumbled for something inside his pocket. Before Jim could see what he pulled out, Aluk gave another sharp command. "Turn around. Look at the wall."

Jim shivered. Was Aluk going to stab him in the back?

He obeyed and Aluk went to the wire door. He worked with the combination lock, but kept his head turned so he could watch Jim. When he had opened the door, he pushed Jim and Mountie into the cage.

With a jeer of satisfaction, the thief closed the door. He snapped the lock and gave the lock dial a twist. For a moment Aluk stood on the other side looking at Mountie, his black eyes greedy but admiring. "You fine dog. I go now, but . . ." He paused and gloated. "But I be back to get you, Mountie."

The fur rose on the husky's neck and he growled. As Aluk turned to go, a small piece of paper fell from beneath his parka and fluttered to the floor.

The cabin door squeaked and Aluk went out into the night.

Chapter 3

"WELL, MOUNTIE," Jim said, "I suppose he's gone back after his gun." Jim turned and walked over to the pile of pelts. "Or maybe he's gone to bring some of his pals to help kidnap you, boy."

Jim sat down on the soft pelts. "At least we have a cozy bed. But what do we use for food?"

Jim thought about his family. He knew they were counting the hours until he came back with the medicine. His parents might even be out doctoring the villagers now while Mary Beth cared for little Sarah.

Or Dad might be seated beside their shortwave receiver, picking out some strange coded message, his favorite winter pastime. Or the family might be reading the Bible together and praying for him. Little did they know how much he needed their prayers.

With that thought, Jim reached into an inner pocket. He pulled out his Testament and began to read from Matthew 6 in the faint light cast by the lantern.

"Your Father knoweth what things ye have need of, before ye ask . . . Therefore I say unto you, take no thought for your life, what ye shall eat, or what ye shall drink; nor yet for your body, what ye shall put on. Is not the life more than meat, and the body more than raiment? Behold, the fowls of the air: for they sow not, neither do they reap . . . yet your heavenly Father feedeth them. Are ye not much better than they?" [2]

He read through the chapter and into the next, "Ask, and it shall be given you; seek, and ye shall find; knock, and it shall be opened unto you . . ." [3]

Jim paused then and looked up at the wire door and the bright new lock. "And it shall be opened unto you." He repeated the words slowly.

Bowing his head, he prayed aloud, "O God, thank You for the Bible and its helpful words. Please, You know how important my journey is to Your work back home. Do make a way for us to get back in time. For Jesus' sake. Amen."

After praying, he moved toward the wire partition and began to inspect it, inch by inch. He could find no way out except through the door, and that was locked.

He began to work at the lock, trying one combination after another, but it wouldn't budge. His wrists became sore from working through the wire fencing.

As he peered through the wire, he noticed the small piece of paper on the floor. "It's funny I didn't notice that before," Jim said. "Aluk must have dropped it."

He yawned. "Looks like a piece of tissue paper or a postage stamp, Mountie, but I guess it won't do us much good. I can't send a letter from here."

He blinked and started to stretch out to sleep but something made him go back and look again at the stamp. In

[2] Matthew 6:25-26
[3] Matthew 7:7

the dim light, Jim thought he saw pencil marks on it. He went closer to the wire. "There's writing on it, Mountie," he said aloud to his dog. "Looks like numbers, but I can't make them out." He stopped and turned to Mountie.

"Say, I wonder if that could be the combination for the lock. Maybe that's why Aluk had me turn toward the wall when he took something out of his pocket. Maybe he was afraid I would see the combination."

Quickly he dropped to the floor and reached through the wire. "Too far," he groaned, trying to reach it.

He felt through his pockets for something. His comb. He tried once again. Almost—only an inch or less. He stretched until the cords in his arm ached. Still he couldn't make it. He felt in his pockets but found nothing else to reach with.

"It might not be the combination written on that stamp, Mountie, but I'd sure like to know. Can't you think of something that will reach, fellow?" Jim spoke desperately.

While he talked, he nervously ran the comb through the dog's shiny coat. The dog's fur crackled and snapped with static electricity. It stood up on end as he brought the comb back for another stroke.

"I've got it—*I've got it!*" he shouted. "Thanks, old fellow."

He began to comb Mountie's coat in earnest. After five or six vigorous strokes, he dove toward the wire and stretched far out. Had he been quick enough? Or had the electricity in the comb faded out? No, the stamp moved. *It moved!* Just a quarter of an inch, but it *had moved.*

He repeated the procedure three more times. At last he had the paper within reach. He dropped the comb and picked up the stamp, his heart beating like a tom-tom. He saw at once that it was the combination! Evidently the stamp had been the only piece of paper Aluk had when he copied down the secret figures.

Excitedly now, Jim worked the dial. "R5 . . . that means turn the dial to the right to number five," he muttered. "R20 . . ." He turned the dial and repeated "20."

There was a lull in the howl of the wind and outside Jim heard a man cough. Aluk was back. "No, no, it can't be! Not yet."

Frantically Jim worked now. L2 . . . L30 . . . R10 . . . *click!*

"Mountie, we're free!"

He stopped short, for the cabin door squeaked and slowly opened. It was Aluk! And he had his rifle.

Jim dropped the lock and flung open the wire door. Mountie, catching the scent of the thief, streaked toward him. Jim froze. There was no stopping Mountie now.

In one mighty bound, the angry dog went for Aluk's throat, hitting him with terrible force and knocking the surprised man hard against the wall. Aluk slumped to the floor with a thud, and the gun slid from his limp hands.

Jim came to life. "Mountie, you haven't . . . you haven't killed him, have you?" he cried hoarsely. Dashing forward, he knelt by the man.

He lifted Aluk's head and pushed back the fur hood. Mountie's teeth had made a nasty gash below Aluk's chin. "He must have hit his head on that wall pretty hard," Jim noted aloud. "But he's still breathing, thank God."

He took a handkerchief from his pocket and made a temporary bandage for the throat wound. Then he went to the door. "Come on, Mountie. Let's rouse the dogs and get going. We'll have to find help or he'll bleed to death."

Outside, Mountie went at once to his task of rousing the dog team as they slept in the snow.

Jim brushed away the snow that covered the sled and moved some of the load to make room for Aluk. A moment later he was harnessing the team. Then he ran inside the cabin to get his patient.

The unconscious Aluk was heavier than he had expected. But the sight of blood oozing through the handkerchief gave Jim superhuman strength to drag Aluk to the sled. Jim covered him with the thick sled robe, and went back in the cabin. Beside the lantern's glow, he studied his wrist compass.

"According to the way Aluk turned to bring us here, Grubstake must be in that direction," he said to himself, pointing straight west.

He blew out the light and groped for the door. Now without that frail yellow gleam it was really dark. The door squeaked behind him.

"Mush! Mush, boys!" he called into the darkness. The dogs strained forward in response, and headed toward what he hoped was Grubstake.

Chapter 4

THE WIND rushed against him with great force. Sometimes it almost took his breath away. Then suddenly it would stop with a taunting silence that told him the wind had circled only to get a better run at him the next time.

It was during one of those lulls, about 15 minutes after he started out, that Jim saw lights. "Look, you malamutes, look! Lights ahead!" he cried.

The dogs began to yelp excitedly as they came to Grubstake's two rows of buildings. From each crude dwelling, small patches of light shone on the snow.

"Let's try this one," Jim called to the team. They seemed thankful for the stop. Each dog, except Mountie, dropped wearily to the ground.

In response to Jim's pounding, the door opened slowly and a stocky man with bushy eyebrows and a heavy mustache filled the doorway. Over his shoulder, a kind-faced woman peered curiously out at Jim.

"Oui . . . oui?" the man grunted.

French, thought Jim. *How am I going to make them understand?* He pointed toward the sled and tried to recall a few words of French.

"L'homme, L'homme—the man—the man. He's mal hurt—bad hurt," stammered Jim.

The man scowled, not quite sure what Jim was trying to say. But behind him, the woman smiled and spoke in broken English. "You—you have man—bad hurt?"

Jim sighed in relief. "Yes. Could you help, please? I'm afraid he might bleed to death."

The woman spoke rapid French to the man who turned to reach for a red woolen jacket that hung by the door.

She faced Jim again and said, "My man help you bring him inside."

Aluk groaned as the two carried him into the warm building. It was then that the Frenchman recognized Aluk. Jim watched the man's eyes narrow and he stepped back in alarm as the man thundered something in French.

His wife, quick to see that Jim could not understand, repeated the words in English. "He say, 'How this happened to Aluk?'" Then softly she added, "Aluk and my man—good friends."

Jim's only answer was a quick move toward Aluk. He bent down and hurriedly began to remove the man's outer clothing. He was aware all the while that the Frenchman was studying him. But Jim breathed easier when finally the burly fellow knelt on the other side of Aluk and started to help.

Aluk began to mumble. He was regaining consciousness. Jim would have to get away fast.

Soon he saw his opportunity. The Frenchman was occupied now with bandaging Aluk's wound. Jim moved to the door and slipped outside.

He darted for the sled yelling, "Mush on, boys! Mush!" as he ran.

The dogs leaped to their feet.

Jim wheeled the team and they fled in the direction they had come. Behind him, he could hear an angry man roaring threats.

"Free at last," Jim reflected, "and on our way." But suddenly he wondered. Was he truly free after all? True, Aluk and the Frenchman were behind. He was out of immediate danger as far as they were concerned. But now he realized that he faced what could be a merciless enemy— an Alaskan blizzard!

The wind was not playing games now. It moaned and whined and drove the snow with such force that it felt like stinging pebbles.

Jim had planned to stop next to Dall City, 40 miles south of Grubstake. But Dall City was about a seven-hour trip even with good sledding. He couldn't hope to reach there alive tonight in this blizzard.

The dogs were tired and had not yet been fed. Jim himself felt the pangs of hunger. But where could they spend the night? He didn't dare take the chance of being found in Grubstake by the Frenchman.

Then it came to him. Why, yes, of course. Back to Aluk's hideout. He wouldn't have a warm stove there, but at least he'd be protected from the storm.

Jim looked back over his shoulder and took his bearings from the dim lights of Grubstake. His earlier tracks had already been wiped out by the high wind and snow. "This should lead us to Aluk's place," he muttered half aloud.

But after traveling some time, they hadn't yet reached the cabin. "Must be there . . . ," he kept telling himself. "We must be."

His eyes watered and smarted. His cheeks were numb.

He had to cover his face with his fur mitten to keep out the cold. Suddenly, they were moving down a slight incline. Then the sled shot ahead. Jim's feet slipped and his heart sank. They were skimming over ice! A river.

The only river around was the Yukon, two or three miles south of Grubstake and Aluk's hideout. He admitted it now. They were lost.

On the opposite side they hit hard snow again. One runner struck a high object and the sled almost turned over. Jim managed to right it in time. But he stumbled and fell. He lay stunned for a moment. Then he realized the dogs and sled had gone on ahead.

Jim stumbled to his feet. "Mountie, Mountie. Stop! Stop! boy, stop!"

He raced desperately after the dogs, stumbling and falling as he went. He felt the sting of frostbite on his cheeks caused by his own heavy breathing. He stopped. "It's no use. There is only one thing to do now." He spoke aloud, and his own voice startled him in the stillness.

He turned and trudged back to the river, feeling carefully along the bank. In a moment he found what he wanted. A deep snowdrift. Dropping wearily to his knees, he burrowed into it with his mittens. After what seemed like a long, long time, he had his "igloo" dug out.

He felt tired . . . so very tired. He huddled there in his snowbank bed and fought to stay awake. As long as he had kept running behind the sled, he hadn't thought of sleep. But now he wanted to sleep more than anything. He wanted to, but didn't dare. If he once fell asleep, he might never wake up. He would not be the first to die by freezing. "Oh, God, keep me awake," he prayed over and over.

Sleep . . . sleep! He could feel himself getting drowsier.

His eyelids felt heavy.

All became quiet and peaceful. He stopped fighting. How good it was to sleep. . . .

Chapter 5

THE WIND seemed to whine again. It was close now. Jim stirred in his half-conscious sleep. The wind seemed to be licking his cheeks.

Then Jim was fully conscious. In one quick movement, he sat straight up. Horror filled him. He couldn't move a muscle. An animal was in his snowdrift shelter. It was too dark to see, but he could sense its presence.

Could it be a prowling timber wolf? It came closer and Jim could feel its warm breath. Gently, the animal nuzzled Jim's shoulder and whined again.

Jim went limp with relief. "Mountie—good old Mountie!" he cried. "You scared me half to death." He hugged his animal friend. Then, realizing he would still be sound asleep if it weren't for Mountie, he hugged him again. "Mountie, God sent you back to wake me up."

Jim guessed that Mountie, having discovered his master was gone, had turned the team around to find him. He hardly dared imagine what had happened to the other dogs. Tangled harness, confusion, overturned sled?

He hoped the dogs hadn't fought. He knew their nerves were brittle from a long day's pull. He knew too that many a driver had lost good dogs at times like this. Huskies had gone mad and slashed each other to death.

If his sled had upset, the dogs would certainly have found the frozen fish he had brought for their feed.

Whatever happened, here was faithful Mountie back again.

Jim started to crawl out of the drift but hurriedly drew back. Outside the storm was fierce. He knew he wouldn't get far. He was weak from hunger and weariness. Mountie would have to go. Maybe he could find help somewhere, somehow. But would help come in time to keep Jim from freezing?

"Mountie, boy, it's up to you. I'm sorry I drove you off the right trail. I thought I could get back to Aluk's hideout. But here we are, lost in a real blizzard. I hate to, but I'll have to send you out into it."

Mountie whined and pranced like an uneasy pony. He seemed to be waiting for an order from Jim that would send him on his way.

"Looks like our only hope, Mountie. Guess you'll have to face that awful storm—" Jim's words trailed off. "That's no good. How would anyone know what you wanted to tell them. They'd think you were just a prowler . . . might even take you for a wolf and shoot." He sank back, discouraged.

"O Lord, O Lord." He wanted to pray for so many things—his mission, the dogs and sled, his father and mother back doctoring the sick Alaskans, Aluk. Yes—Aluk too—and himself and Mountie. All these. But the prayer seemed to come only from deep in his heart. All he could say was "O Lord—O Lord."

"Your Father knoweth what things ye have need of,

before ye ask Him." The words burned in his mind. "Your Father knoweth . . ." [4]

If only his mind would clear so he could think. He was trying to remember something his dad had told him. What was it? Lying there in the snow, he began to doze again . . . to dream? A compass in his hand.

A compass. That was it. He shook himself awake. "Mountie, a compass—my wrist compass. Here, hold still while I fasten it to your harness. It's a sign that a white man is lost. Eskimos never use a compass. God helped me remember that, I'm sure."

Mountie bounded a few feet away, then came back whining. Twice he did it.

"No, I'm not going this time, fellow. You go find help," Jim ordered.

The husky turned obediently into the swirling snow and was gone.

Once again Jim realized he was not only weary and lonely, but also very hungry. He felt weak and dizzy. He remembered trying to pray again—for Mountie. Then it was quiet and restful, just as before. So quiet and restful . . .

Jim had no idea how much time had passed when he began to hear a great choir of voices. Beautiful lights appeared and disappeared. He seemed to float through the air, light as a balloon.

What queer sensations! Odd-looking creatures appeared beside him. They reached out and hit his face . . . darted away, then came back to hit again. They began to pound his chest, his arms, his legs. They started to talk. What

---

[4] Matthew 6:8

lusty voices they had for such little fellows. And how their slaps stung. Why were they beating him?

"Yaka wind chako halo?" asked one. It seemed so far away . . . yet so very near. "Yaka wind chako halo?" it asked again.

Jim recognized those queer-sounding words now. That was the Eskimo way of asking if he were still alive, or "if his breath was gone." He blinked.

Evidently Eskimos were trying to revive him. He could hear them chattering all around. Gradually he realized what had happened. Mountie had succeeded—and in time!

Then it seemed as if he were back floating through the air again.

"You sleep long sleep—that good." An Eskimo man smiled down at Jim. Mountie nosed closer to his young master.

Jim tried to sit up, but his head was spinning. "Where am I?" he asked thickly. "How did I get here?"

"You with friends," replied the same Eskimo in English. Jim noted that the man looked strong and kind, and was about his father's age. Jim looked around. He was in a large Eskimo igloo. Half a dozen Eskimos squatted around, smiling and nodding in a friendly way.

They all talked at once now that Jim was awake. Some got up and went outside. Two women entered, each carrying something.

"Muckamuck . . . Muckamuck skookum muckamuck."

Jim understood that. "Good grub," he repeated in English, "and am I starved!"

The Eskimo man laughed as Jim reached to take the food. "Thank you, thank you," Jim said.

"You thank good God up there that you live." The Eskimo pointed skyward.

"Are you a Christian . . . ah, ah . . . what is your name?" Jim asked.

"Skoolumakumkum is my name, but they call me Skoo."

"Mine is Jim."

"All of us Christians," the Eskimo said. "Kind white doctor name of Peterson. He tell us about God one time when all tribe have fever. He give us medicine and tell about God who loves us."

"Did you say *Peterson?*" Jim interrupted him.

The Eskimo nodded.

"That's my name—Jim Peterson." Jim was too excited to eat, starved though he was. "That must have been my father, Hugh Peterson."

"That's right."

As he began to eat, Jim listened to the Eskimo's tale of how Jim's dad had befriended them some years before. Now, unexpectedly, his life had been saved because of the Gospel his Dad had preached years before.

He realized again just how important his mission to Fairbanks was. It might be the means of physically saving the natives of Nolan. But more important, it would offer Dad opportunities to tell them how to be saved spiritually.

The women brought in more food.

It was strange looking. Jim hesitated. But he did not want to hurt their feelings, so he accepted it.

"Try it," Skoo encouraged.

"What is it?" Jim asked politely.

"A real treat," replied Skoo. "It's raw frozen bone marrow from caribou leg bones. Good."

Jim nibbled a little. "Say, it's not bad. In fact, it's *really* good!" He ate until his hunger was satisfied.

"You feel better now," Skoo said, smiling. "Did you know you sleep for 14 hours?"

"Fourteen hours!" Jim repeated. "I must have been pretty far gone when you found me."

"It's good thing you thought to send that compass with your dog. At first, we throw fish to him. He don't even smell it. Then he come inside igloo, and we see compass."

All the rest of the day was spent in repairing the chewed harness. After hearing Jim's story, the Eskimos had gone out and found Jim's sled. Mountie had helped round up every dog of the team.

Jim stayed that night with his new friends. They talked, and Jim told them of his trip. He read chapter after chapter for them from his pocket Testament. They were eager to hear the stories of Jesus again.

That night, before snuggling down in their individual sleeping bags, they knelt in a circle and asked Jim to pray.

"Thank You, dear God, for bringing us safely this far," he said. "Thank You for sending these good people along in time to save my life. Bless them and help them grow in their Christian lives. In Jesus' name I pray. Amen."

By the next morning the blizzard had spent itself and Jim prepared to leave. "Have to make up for lost time, won't we, Mountie?"

"Wait," said Skoo. He disappeared into the igloo. Soon he came out carrying a container of water steaming in the cold air. In his other hand he had a small piece of fur.

"What are you going to do?" Jim asked.

"Turn sled over," Skoo instructed. "This makes sled go easy."

Jim watched as Skoo dipped the fur into the water and

ran it quickly over the ivory-shod runners. In the sub-zero weather the water froze almost instantly, forming a hard ice coating on each runner.

"Oh, I see," Jim marvelled. "Kind of a grease job." As he watched, the Eskimo applied two more coats.

The sled skimmed rapidly over the snow now. Jim turned to wave a final good-bye to his rescuers. Completely rested, he headed the team south, back onto the trail to Fairbanks.

Chapter 6

THE WEATHER was ideal now. Mountie led the team on, head high and alert. For three days after leaving the Eskimos, Jim drove the team and found shelter at night as he had mapped out.

On the fourth day, he shouted, "There it is, huskies! Fairbanks!" As they swung up the main street, Jim responded to the friendly waves of a group of children in bright parkas.

"That's a neat team you've got there!" one of the boys said. "Look at that lead dog!"

"Thank you," said Jim. "Maybe you could tell me where I can board the dogs for the night."

"Sure thing." The boy pointed out the direction. Jim found the place. He left the team, all except Mountie, and went to find a hotel room for the night.

"I want to get cleaned up a little before we go to the doctor's office to see about the supplies," he said to Mountie.

Half a block off the main street he found a hotel. He walked in and signed the register. The clerk hesitated, then said, "You planning to take your dog in too?"

"If Mountie can't stay, I don't," replied Jim.

"Well." The clerk smiled. "It's a little unusual. But I can see you have a pretty valuable dog there." He winked at Jim and added, "I think I'd do the same, especially with all the stealing going on lately. Your room is right down the hallway, third door around the corner."

Jim thanked him and walked toward his room, Mountie at his side. As they turned the corner, Mountie sniffed the carpet, and the fur along his neck stood up. He stiffened and growled.

"What's the matter, boy? I thought you reserved that kind of a growl for Aluk." Jim laughed. "And he's miles behind us." He turned the key in the lock and opened the door. "You first, Mr. Mountie."

After a quick washup, Jim said, "C'mon, boy. Let's get over to the doctor's office, so he can work on the order tonight. We're running behind schedule."

At the doctor's office, Jim introduced himself and explained the urgency of his trip. He handed the doctor the list of needed drugs.

"Hmmmm." The doctor frowned. "You must have quite a serious situation up there at Nolan. I'll do my best and work as late as necessary tonight so you can pick up the medicine early tomorrow."

Turning to leave, Jim said, "Thanks, Doctor. I'll be here first thing in the morning. Good night."

As he left the office and walked down a long hall leading to the street, Jim noticed a man hurrying ahead of him. Something about the man's actions made Jim suspicious. Then he remembered that the man hadn't been standing in the hall when he and Mountie went in. And the only other door was an outside one.

Strange, Jim thought. *He acts like a peeping Tom. He couldn't have been trying to hear the conversation with the Doc, surely. Why would he want to? Probably had an appointment with the doctor and lost his nerve.*

He opened the door to the street and slapped Mountie's side. "How about a good steak supper, Mountie? Then we'll turn in for some sleep. We have to get an early start in the morning."

* * *

It was still dark in the morning when Jim threw back the covers and rolled out of bed. "Have to wash . . . breakfast . . . harness the team . . . meet the doctor . . . load the supplies . . . ," he said to his dog.

Faint streaks of light colored the sky as Jim halted the team at the doctor's office.

Jim stepped into the office and saw a neat stack of boxes piled by the door. "Good morning, Doctor," he called, but got no answer. He listened, then frowned. "He must be here," Jim muttered. "The door is unlocked and the lights are on." Then Jim heard muffled voices coming from a back room. "Hello!" He called louder.

"Just one minute," a voice called back. Jim was puzzled. That wasn't the doctor's voice. He heard footsteps and a man about 30 years old stepped into the room.

He was thin and slightly balding. His white teeth flashed beneath a bushy mustache. He wore a doctor's coat which was wrinkled and smudged.

"You are Mr. Peterson," he said, extending a hand toward Jim. "I—I am Dr. Lavel . . . assistant to Dr. Wallace, whom you met yesterday."

"Yes, I—then I guess you know why I'm here?" Jim asked.

"Dr. Wallace informed me that you would pick up the medicine . . . It's all ready for you."

Just then a thump from the back room made them both glance at the door. "What was that?" Jim asked.

"Oh . . . that . . . that—" Dr. Laval coughed. "That, er, I have a sick dog which gave me a lot of trouble." He grinned broadly and pointed to his soiled coat. "Now, the money."

Jim thought the doctor seemed rather impatient, but said nothing about it. "Yes, I have the signed check my dad sent with me. He didn't know what the cost would be—somewhere around $250, he thought. I'll make it out if you have a pen, please."

Leading Jim to the office desk, Dr. Laval handed him a pen stating, "Make it out for $500." He grinned at Jim.

"Five hundred dol . . ." Jim stopped short. "Why?"

"Do you not realize, my boy, that these drugs are hard to get up here in Alaska? They just doubled in price. So sorry, but—"

"So sorry! You can say that for me too," Jim spoke thoughtfully. "Poor Dad's pocketbook. But I can't waste time arguing about money with people's lives depending on me."

Producing the check, Jim reached for the pen.

"Make it out to Dr. Maurice Laval." The man spoke quickly.

Something about the fellow didn't ring true to Jim. He paused before writing. As he glanced over the desk, his eyes rested on a letterhead. The only name on it was the name of the other doctor. He made out the check to W. B. Wallace, M.D. just as it appeared on the letterhead, and handed it to the man in white.

Dr. Laval scowled. "That's not the right name."

"I'm sorry," Jim said. "But Dr. Wallace is the man I placed the order with, so I think he should get the check. If you and he are partners, I'm sure—"

A thump from the back room made Dr. Laval fold the check quickly and place it in his wallet. "OK," he said nervously, "it is fine. Your boxes are ready there by the door. I have to leave now—have a call to make." He smiled again. "Have a good trip home."

Jim had the sled loaded in a short time. He threw the fur robe over the boxes and shouted to the team. "We're off, huskies! Mush!"

As the last buildings disappeared behind him, Jim bowed his head and asked God to give him a safe return trip.

The sun peeped through a gray sky. It made Jim's heart leap for joy. He burst into the chorus, "Heavenly Sunshine," singing loudly as the team moved along. It was good to have God's sunshine flooding his heart.

They sped on, hour after hour, making good time. It was late afternoon and they were not far now from the town of Brooks when Jim heard the drone of an airplane, drawing closer and closer. Soon Jim spotted it straight behind him. "Sure is flying low," he said.

Two minutes later it zoomed over his head, flying at about 100 feet. He watched it gain altitude sharply, pull into a lazy bank and circle back. "It's acting kinda funny, don't you think, huskies?" he said aloud to the dogs.

The plane was behind him again. This time it came much lower.

Jim noticed, with concern, that the plane did not rise. It settled down on the snow ahead and stopped.

The cabin door opened. Out of the plane sprang three grim-faced men—Aluk, the Frenchman, and Dr. Laval.

It was suddenly clear now—Mountie's strange behavior in the hotel hallway, the "peeping Tom" at the doctor's office, Dr. Laval's demand for extra money.

Aluk and the Frenchman must have flown to Fairbanks ahead of him. They were in the hotel where he had stayed. Mountie had scented them. Of course, this "Dr." Laval was mixed up with the other two—all partners in crime.

Aluk spoke. "So we meet again! You not take Mountie now—I fix you."

"What do you want?" Jim asked.

"We won't delay you long," Dr. Laval said.

The three men held a short mumbled conference. Then Aluk went back to the plane. Laval and the Frenchman stepped toward the sled. The Frenchman threw off the robe and started to lift one of the boxes. Jim's heart sank as he carried the medicine to the plane.

"Just a minute!" Jim spoke rapidly. "That medicine has been bought and paid for—at your price too."

"We are only helping you," replied Laval.

"Helping me. Looks like you're helping yourself," Jim retorted.

"But we are going to help you get the medicine to Nolan faster. We will fly it much faster that you could deliver it. Of course, your father will be delighted to pay . . ."

"Pay," broke in Jim. "I've paid plenty already."

"You misunderstand," Laval interrupted. "We are only charging for the extra fast delivery. I'm sure it should be worth, say $1,000."

So that was their scheme. First they steal the medicine, then sell it at about twice its price. Now they planned to collect another thousand. It would take every penny of Dad's savings. But he knew Dad would pay because he needed it so badly.

Jim's heart raced as he watched. Something had to be done. If only he could think of some way to keep these fellows from taking off just long enough to get help. Brooks was less than an hour away. Yet with three armed men around him, what could he do?

"Thees time I take what I want." It was Aluk. "Here, take thees rope . . . tie Mountie good."

Chapter 7

JIM FELT SICK. Bind Mountie with ropes for a guy who
didn't have the nerve to do it himself? Never! Just then he
noticed something the others hadn't. Mountie was quiet.
With Aluk so close, that wasn't natural. He shot a quick
glance at the big husky. His heart leaped, Mountie was
quietly gnawing his harness straps. The dog needed only
a little more time.

Jim reached for the rope Aluk handed him. Could he
stall long enough? He dropped it clumsily, and, with a
clever twist, snarled it at the same time.

"Dumb keed!" roared Aluk. "Peek eet op."

Jim stooped to obey, chancing another glance at
Mountie.

The husky had already started his run. Jim held his
breath. He'd have to be quick. Now was his chance to get
to the plane. Suddenly the air was filled with a mixture of
wild shouts and barking. Just as Mountie hit Aluk's
shoulder, Jim saw Laval go for his revolver. *"Crack."* Hot
lead whined over his head.

Had that bullet passed through his faithful husky? The
answer came fast. Mountie and Aluk were thrashing in the

snow. The dog's teeth flashing and snapping—the man struggling and yelling.

Laval stood watching, waiting for the husky to separate himself from Aluk long enough for another shot.

Jim seized the rope. With all the power he could summon, he made a flying tackle for Laval's legs, and the man sprawled in the snow. His gun landed six feet away in the snow.

Furiously now Jim wound the rope around Laval's legs. "Mountie! Mountie!" Jim yelled, calling him off. Aluk was cowering with fear. As long as Mountie stood near, Jim knew he wouldn't have to worry about that rascal.

As Jim finished tying Laval, the Frenchman came running from the plane with a rifle. But before he could use it, Mountie had him at bay too.

Jim scrambled for Laval's revolver. Blowing the snow out of it, he shouted, "OK, throw that rifle down."

"Oui, oui," promised the Frenchman, his eyes wide with fear. "Le dog . . . le dog . . ."

"I'll hold him. Here, Mountie."

The husky quieted, but stood alert as the Frenchman dropped his rifle.

"Bring it here, Mountie, atta boy," Jim ordered.

Mountie obediently gripped the stock of the gun between his teeth.

Jim took the rifle from Mountie and put it on the empty sled.

"Up, boys," he spoke. "Mush now, mush."

Mountie, although not in the harness, took his position at the head of the string. Jim swung the team up past the plane a few yards, then stopped.

All three men watched, swearing and shaking their fists,

but not daring to attempt any action now. Jim was sizing up the situation in his mind.

S'pose I could load the medicine back onto the sled? But Aluk and the Frenchman might try something while my back is turned. No, I think I'll do something else. If I don't, I'll have to deal with these fellows all the way home.

He lifted the revolver and stepped closer to the plane, firing four shots at the motor. A spark plug shattered and the copper gas line snapped in two places. Gas trickled out.

"There, guess that'll keep 'em grounded till we can get back here with the law from Brooks. I'll leave the boxes in the plane so Aluk and his friends can be taken with the stolen goods." He turned and dashed toward the sled, dropping the gun beside the rifle on the sled. "OK, boys, let's be on our way . . . mush!"

As he pulled away, he looked back to see Aluk and the Frenchman run to inspect the damaged plane. Laval was still on the ground struggling with the ropes.

The huskies seemed to sense the need for speed. They streaked along as Mountie set the pace. Jim prayed earnestly as he ran and rode in turn. If his mission was going to count now, God would have to work it out.

It was growing steadily darker. Would he be able to reach help before those men behind him could make repairs?

They sped along for about 45 minutes. Then Jim heard it. An airplane motor, faint but real. It grew stronger as it came closer. "It can't be them!" He felt sick. "It just can't be."

But when the plane flew over, it wasn't quite dark out. No mistake. Jim could see that it was the bandit's plane.

They must have had a repair kit along.

Jim suddenly felt defeated and very tired. Had God forsaken him?

It was dark when he entered the small town of Brooks. He headed for a building with the sign "Police—City Hall" on it.

He tried the door. It opened into a warm, well-lighted room, with an elbow-high counter running the width of the room. A square-jawed giant of a man looked up pleasantly from the other side of the counter.

"Hi, there!" the man said. "New 'round these parts, aren't you?" Extending a huge hand, he said, "I'm Captain Scott, Alaska Police."

Quickly, Jim told his story, not forgetting to mention Dr. Wallace. He had begun to wonder if the kind doctor had been injured. As he talked, Jim noticed something across the room. The sight of it made him stop. The law officer, who had been taking notes, looked up.

"What's the matter, Son?" he asked.

"Oh, excuse me." Jim apologized. "I—just noticed your shortwave radio transmitter there, it could—I mean—couldn't we get through to Nolan with it? My dad has a receiving set. He turns it on every night about this time."

"That's a good idea. Just one catch—did you happen to notice whether this Aluk's plane carried a radio?"

"Yes, it did," Jim said.

"I'm afraid to risk it then. They might pick up the message in the plane, and that would spoil everything." The officer paused. "You see, we've suspected these fellows for some time, especially in connection with smuggling stolen furs into Canada and the United States. But we've never been able to catch them with the goods." He paused a moment, thinking. "This would be our chance, though, if only we could arrange some kind of a code."

"You mean, so Dad could keep them until you got there?"

"Well, I wasn't thinking of myself," the officer said. "But I happen to know that a couple of F.B.I. men flew up to Fort Hamlin, just yesterday, to see if they could crack this smuggling case."

The two stood thinking. Then the officer spoke again.

"If only we could think of some subject entirely foreign to those bandits. Even then, we're only hoping that your father would be tuned in."

Jim thought hard. One thing they wouldn't know much about was the Word of God. "I've got it," he said. "What about a Bible code? Dad would be sure to be curious, and figure it out, too. He's good at figuring out codes."

"Say, that's a great idea," the officer said. "You work it out while I try to contact the F.B.I. agents at Fort Hamlin. Here, come and sit down while I put in a call to Fairbanks and have them check on Dr. Wallace."

Chapter 8

FOR 15 minutes the two of them sat, Captain Scott at the transmitter, Jim at a desk, deep in thought. Jim was trying to figure out how to start the code. He was glad now for the times he and Dad had played around with codes on long winter evenings. He thumbed through his New Testament.

What he'd have to do, he decided, would be to use separated verses. He was sure Aluk and his friends didn't have a Bible, in case they should pick up the code.

Finally Jim hit on an idea. He picked up a pencil and worked feverishly, hope renewing his energy. He turned the pages of his Testament and wrote.

"Got something?" Captain Scott asked.

"Yup. The old wheels upstairs finally started moving," Jim said, pointing to his head.

"Dr. Wallace is OK. A patient had found him tied up in a back room. And the F.B.I. men from Fort Hamlin will be here in 45 minutes or less," Captain Scott said. Then he smiled. "And you are going to fly home."

"Fly home!" Jim cried.

"Yep, I contacted Fort Hamlin. They're flying down here

48

to pick up you and your team. Then you'll head for Nolan right away."

"That means I'll be home tonight!" Jim cried.

"That means you'll land in Nolan only an hour or so behind those three bandits. You'll be there for the arrest. Guess you'd better get back to that code now."

Ten minutes later Jim handed Captain Scott a sheet of paper. "There it is, Captain."

Captain Scott took the paper and studied it carefully. Jim explained the code system.

The policeman turned to the transmitter. "*Isaac to Abraham . . . Isaac to Abraham.*" Over and over again, he gave the greeting. Jim sat quietly by, praying.

Captain Smith's voice boomed on.

"Genesis 1:1 *In the beginning . . .*"

He continued the message, giving the numeral first and then the reference that went with it. It would be tricky for Dad at first, but simple once he figured out the key. And knowing Dad, Jim was sure he would.

The policeman went on and on: "1. John 1:14; 5:3; 15:20 . . . 2. John 1:12; 1:14; 3:4; 5:45; 5:3; 2:18; 4:40 . . . 3. John 15:13; 4:20; 4:15 . . . 4. John 5:28; 14:17; 5:45; 5:3; 4:29; 5:3; 3:4; 14:17 . . . 5. John 5:45; 4:20; 3:4; 2:18 . . . 6. John 14:1; 14:17; 2:18 . . . 7. John 14:17; 4:40; 4:29; 1:14; 14:27; 14:17 . . . 8. John 14:23; 5:3; 5:28."

* * *

Back at Nolan, Mary Beth and her mother patiently waited for Dr. Peterson to return. He had been gone most of the day, taking the last of the medicine with him. They had prayed for both him and Jim. Now baby Sarah was in bed and Mary Beth turned on the radio to keep them company.

An hour later Dr. Peterson came in, tired and pale. "Looks like you've picked up my hobby, listening to the shortwave radio," he said, smiling at Mary Beth.

"Daddy, I've been listening to it for the last hour," she said. "It's funny. They're using Scripture. Mom heard it too."

"Scripture? In a code?" he said.

"Yes. Not the usual dot-dash either. This was a voice," Mother added.

"Bible code! That's a funny one," Hugh Peterson said, going over to the receiver.

"I copied it down," Mary Beth said, handing him a paper. "You and Jim like to work them out; so we thought you'd want to see this."

He studied the paper. "Isaac to Abraham. That's plain —sender to receiver. Let's see, Isaac and Abraham . . . two Old Testament Bible characters—Abraham, Isaac's father," he mumbled. "Son to Father!"

Suddenly, he turned to his wife. "Are you thinking what I'm thinking? This code could have been beamed at us. Jim may be in trouble."

Reaching for his Bible, he said, "The code is all taken from the book of John."

"We noticed that too—all except the first verse, Genesis 1:1," Mother said.

"Then that's our key," Mr. Peterson put in.

Three heads leaned over the Bible, puzzling over the first verse.

"The first three words of that verse were repeated as part of the message. I wonder why?" Mrs. Peterson asked, looking troubled.

"The sender seems to be emphasizing the figure 1. Genesis is the first book, first chapter, first verse . . . 'In the beginning' . . . or first . . ." Dad said.

"Could it mean the first word in each verse given?" Mary Beth asked suddenly.

They tried it but it didn't make sense.

"It must mean the first letter." A—I—R. Eagerly they worked it out.

"*Air bandits got medicine. Don't let escape. Jim.*"

The Petersons looked at each other, horrified.

"There's no question about it. God directed you to take down that code," Dad said to Mary Beth.

"Listen!" exclaimed his wife. "I hear an airplane."

They rushed to the window. Sure enough a plane was circling the village.

* * *

The twin-engine craft carrying Jim, his dogs, and the F.B.I. agents zoomed along, covering a distance in minutes that would have taken Jim and the team days.

"We should be in Nolan in another 20 minutes," one of the F.B.I. men spoke up.

Jim was tense with excitement. "Pretty nice ride, eh, Mountie?" he asked his dog. He looked at the controls. "We're doing 310 miles per hour."

"Hope your dad was able to decode your message," the F.B.I. agent at the controls said anxiously. "Be too bad if those thieves would escape."

Jim quietly offered up another prayer.

It wasn't long after, that the plane began to lose altitude. Jim watched one of the men bring a powerful searchlight into play.

"There's the mission," shouted Jim, spotting it in the light. "There's home, Mountie, boy."

"Yes . . . and there's something else down there," broke in the F.B.I. man handling the light, "the plane we've been looking for. We'll have to proceed with caution."

The agent brought the plane down skillfully and taxied up to the other plane.

They scattered and approached the house with guns drawn. Jim waited tensely with Mountie by the planes.

One of the men reached a lighted window and peered in. "It's OK," he called, motioning them to come. Jim rushed to the house, Mountie at his heels. They all crowded inside and Jim just stood there taking in the scene before him, a wide grin spreading over his face.

Aluk, Laval, and the Frenchman were seated in the center of the room, surrounded by a group of Eskimos.

"Welcome, folks," Hugh Peterson said, grinning. Mrs. Peterson rushed up and hugged Jim. "Thank the Lord, you're safe," she cried.

Jim grinned. "You got the message then OK?"

"Not so fast—not so fast," his dad said, laughing. "Come on inside, all of you. You too, Mountie."

One of the F.B.I. agents spoke up. "Congratulations on a fine piece of work, sir. We're not used to walking into a completed assignment. Thanks to you and your alert son."

Mr. Peterson smiled. "I deserve no credit. My daughter took down the message," he said, turning to a shy Mary Beth standing in a doorway. "And I'm very proud of Jim."

"Yes, it was a lucky break that he thought of that Bible code message," replied the government agent.

"Lucky break?" asked Hugh Peterson. "No, I don't think it was a lucky break. I believe it came as an answer to prayer."

"What do you mean?" the agent said.

"Just this. We've been praying earnestly that somehow God would arrange for the medicine to get back here before we had planned. We used the last of it today. The epidemic is worse. But in spite of everything, the medicine arrived early."

Jim was bursting with questions. "Say, Dad," he interrupted. "How did you capture these fellows?" He pointed to the prisoners.

"Easy," said his dad. "We rang the chapel bell just as the bandits started to land. Fortunately most of the Eskimo men are well now. They came at once and were here waiting to give these three a surprise party."

The two F.B.I. men strode toward Aluk and his companions. They clipped on three pairs of handcuffs.

The captors and the captives moved toward the door. "We're flying these men to Fairbanks tonight," one of the agents said. "But we'll be back up here as soon as possible for the stolen plane."

"Stolen plane?" Jim asked in surprise.

"Yes, the plane this trio were using was stolen about three weeks ago from Canada." The agent paused, then continued. "We're going to ask one more favor of you, Jim. When we come back, we'd like you to fly down with us and point out Aluk's hideout. Our men have never been able to locate it."

"OK," Jim said, glad to help the F.B.I. again.

Jim and his dad went out to the plane with the men to get their dogs and sled, then returned to a hot supper.

While they ate, Jim told his family the whole story.

"You certainly had a great adventure, Son," his father said at the end.

"Yes," Jim said. He leaned down and stroked Mountie's silver fur. "And I learned through it all that God does direct the path of the Christian."

THE
MYSTERIOUS
CAMEL
OF INDIA

Grace Vernon

Chapter 1

JOE FOSTER stared until his blue eyes fairly popped out of his head. His father had laid a little pile of 10-rupee notes on the carved brass table. He had smoothed the money out carefully, and now he picked up a pair of scissors.

"What on earth are you going to do, Dad?" Joe asked.

"There are no banks in our small town," his father explained. He calmly cut the small pile of bills in half. "This money has to last us two months. If anything happens to it, we'll have nothing to live on."

"Why don't you hide it?"

His father laughed. "Impossible! Even locks and keys aren't much against thieves who can open a Yale lock with a bent pin. No, this is the only way."

Mr. Foster wrapped the pile of half-notes in a sheet of paper and stuffed them into a brass jar on the table.

"If your mother weren't away in Bombay, I'd give her these halves. But since she's gone I'll hide them in this jar and carry the other halves in my pocket. When I need to spend a bill, I'll just stick two matching halves together with clear tape."

"And in the meantime it won't do any good to rob you!" Joe's blue eyes began to sparkle. "That's clever, Dad."

"There are many thieves here—professionals," Mr. Foster went on. "You'll have to get used to seeing things stolen. These people don't see anything wrong with stealing. The only thing to do about them, really, is to bring them to the Lord Jesus Christ and let Him change them."

Joe set his jaw and wondered. When he was little, he had not been able to bear the hot plains of India. He had had to stay in the United States since 1940 with his grandparents while his missionary parents lived in India.

Now, at 12, he was with his parents for the first time. Everything in India—the customs, the people, even his parents—seemed strange and unreasonable to him at times.

His father stepped out onto the veranda to talk with a native Christian. The Indian had stood there, coughing politely instead of knocking. Joe wandered out to the tree outside the bungalow wall where Lal, the camel, was tied.

Joe had begun to like the large beast with its funny, wise face and its huge hump that shook all over like warm jelly when the camel moved. It was an unusually fine animal. Joe's dad said that he had paid a large price for it.

The camel was kneeling by the thorn hedge that fenced the compound, munching the sharp thorns.

Joe went over and patted the stiff curly hair on Lal's neck. The beast only glanced at him in a bored way. Then it went on with its strange meal of thorns. An Indian boy, wearing a huge pinkish turban, had been sitting on the sand watching him. Now he got up and came toward Joe.

"My name Nathoo," he volunteered in English. "You Joe? I knowing secret about this camel."

But he would not tell what it was. And Joe had no time to urge him, because just then he heard his father calling.

It crossed Joe's mind, as he ran toward the veranda, that he had never seen his father look so happy as he did then. Mr. Foster's eyes were sparkling, and the tired-lines of his face had smoothed out.

"A wonderful thing has happened!" he told Joe quietly. "N'rain Singh here has brought good news. The Ranee—that's a real queen, Joey, who lives not far from here—has recovered from a serious illness. She was treated at a mission hospital at Miraj. She wants to give us her jewels. We're to sell them and start a fund to build a mission hospital here."

"Dad, that's great!" Joe exclaimed. Foɪ an instant he felt as if he had stepped into one of the Arabian Nights' tales and gotten lost there. He could just see the jewels—emeralds and diamonds and rubies. "When will you get them?"

"She wants the gift kept quiet, if possible," Mr. Foster said. "Her husband is not a Christian and might not approve. A secret meeting has been arranged an hour from now. N'rain Singh and I must leave at once."

"But, Dad, where will we hide the jewels?" Joe whispered, looking around.

For an instant, Mr. Foster's face clouded with worry. "We'll think of a plan when we return, Joe. In the meantime, don't say anything to anyone about this, understand?"

Joe nodded, his eyes big as saucers. Real jewels! Wow! After his dad left with N'rain Singh, Joe sat down in the shade of the veranda. How about burying the jewels? No, that would hardly do. Probably all the thieves in the area would soon know that the jewels had been given to the missionary for the hospital. They would immediately look any place where the earth was disturbed. To hide the jewels under the floor tiles would be useless too, because that would show plainly.

Joe got up and began to walk slowly around the compound, trying to look casual. The palm trees, the passion vine, the tall white canna flowers offered no place to hide the jewels.

But the old well—how about that? The water level was quite low now. Couldn't the jewels be wrapped up, weighted with a stone, and sunk in the well until it was time to fish them out?

As Joe turned away from the well, he saw something that made him hurry toward the bungalow. The boy Nathoo was standing on the veranda with his nose pressed against the living room window, staring in.

"What do you want?" Joe called as he reached the steps.

The boy turned quickly. His dark eyes seemed to brighten at the sight of Joe. "What are you doing, young sahib?" he asked.

"I've been looking around," Joe said, sitting down in a long chair and watching the Indian boy. "How do you know English?"

"I going mission school two years. Your father teaching me."

"Are you a Christian?" Joe asked.

Nathoo shook his head. "No, no, I cannot be Christian." And as if he didn't want to talk anymore about it, he walked swiftly to the edge of the veranda. Then he turned back to say, "Your camel belonging someone else, young sahib, before your father."

"Of course he did," Joe answered. "Dad didn't raise him." He stared after Nathoo. Why had the boy told him something he already knew? Had he meant more than he seemed to? Joe screwed up his forehead as he puzzled over Nathoo's remark.

Chapter 2

AND THAT'S how Mr. Foster found Joe when he returned with a basket of books in his arms. He took Joe into the bedroom, pulled the curtains, and closed the door.

Together, they removed the books. Inside one was a cleverly concealed compartment where the jewels had been hidden. They took out lovely ornaments of silver and turquoise; nose rings set with pearls and rubies; heavy gold bangles; and emerald earrings.

"They're beautiful, Dad," Joe whispered. He looked up to find his father staring into space. "Why, you're not even looking at them!"

His father smiled. "I guess I was thinking of the new hospital, Son. That will be even more beautiful than these jewels. Tomorrow I can get a train to Bombay and sell them there. In the meantime, pray that they will be safe."

Joe told him about the well, and Mr. Foster agreed that it would be a good hiding place. They wrapped the book containing the jewels in a dark, waterproof sack, then checked the compound to make sure no one was watching them.

When it was almost dark, they lowered the package

down, down into the well, then dropped the cord, package and all, into the water.

After hiding the jewels, Mr. Foster dug near the veranda to make it look as if the jewels had been buried there.

That night Joe dreamed of beautiful queens and finding hidden treasures. Suddenly he awoke with fear gripping him! The soft blackness of the tropical night closed in. For an instant, he was not sure what the blackness hid. Where was he? The dream still seemed so real.

Then a single sound—like a cry that was suddenly choked off—brought him wide awake. He knew where he was, and he knew what that cry meant. Something was wrong!

He jumped out of bed and groped toward the door in the dark, calling, "Dad! Dad!"

By the time he reached the door, his father was out in the hall with his flashlight.

Together they followed the pale circle of light down the tiled hall and out into the living room. Joe watched in bewilderment as the flashlight found first the spot where the blue sofa had been, next the place where Mr. Foster's battered desk had stood.

"They've cleared out the whole living room!" Joe was stunned. "Do you think they knew about the jewels, Dad?"

"Yes," Mr. Foster nodded slowly. "In spite of our precautions, the thieves must have discovered we had the jewels. Now everything's gone. And so quickly that we never heard a sound!"

"But someone did cry out, Dad. I heard him."

"Let's see if anyone is outside, Joe."

Joe followed his father to the door. "Say, Dad, the brass jar is gone, so they must have gotten your cut halves of the 10-rupee notes. How will you buy your train ticket?"

"Without them I can't." Mr. Foster stepped out on the veranda and swept the beam over the floor and the nearby earth. No one was around.

He shone the beam on a spot where the surface of the sand was disturbed. It looked as if something had been dragged over it.

"They didn't get all the furniture away by dragging it," Mr. Foster said. "Yet I can't understand those tracks on the sand. They weren't made by a rickshaw or a bullock cart, or anything else with wheels or runners. See how rough those parallel marks are!"

Together Joe and his father followed the tracks through the loose sand of the compound. The strange trail led in and out among the bushes and flower beds to the road outside the thorn hedge. It ended abruptly.

Joe looked up at his father's face, pale and troubled in the faint glow of the flashlight. "Do you think they got the jewels?"

His father shook his head. "I don't think so. They wouldn't have taken all that furniture unless they thought the jewels might be hidden in it."

Joe glanced at the eastern sky. It was beginning to glow with the faint silver light of dawn.

His father noticed too. "I think we'd better check the well before it gets lighter and make sure the jewels are there," Mr. Foster said. "Then I'll take them to Bombay by camel."

"It will be a dangerous trip for you, Dad."

"I'll be safe, Son. Remember that we've prayed about the jewels. I believe we'll get them to Bombay and turn them into a fund for the hospital. I won't start early because that might make someone suspicious. I'll saddle the camel at the time I usually make my trip to the village near here, and start off. Then instead of coming home, I'll just keep on going to Bombay."

Chapter 3

JOE'S TRIP down the ancient stone-walled well was a new experience. In the darkness, he climbed into the big cold bucket. Then his father lowered him slowly down until his outstretched hand felt the water. Now, in the middle of the dry season, the water was quite low. He had little trouble finding the cord attached to the bundle they had dropped in the day before.

"It's here, Dad," he called softly.

Back up on the ground, he handed the dripping package to his father.

The sky was faintly gray when they reached the house. "Do you think anybody saw us?" Joe asked.

"I hope not. We'll go to bed now and try to sleep until it gets light."

Joe went to bed, but not to sleep. His thoughts were racing. The thieves must be after the jewels. But how had they found out about them so soon? One person had been on the compound when N'rain Singh told Mr. Foster about them—the boy in the pinkish turban, Nathoo.

"If he comes around again, I'll chase him away," Joe decided.

Joe had a good chance to carry out his threat. When his father called him to breakfast he saw Nathoo sitting on the steps, waiting. When Joe went to the door, Nathoo glanced quickly at him. Then he looked back at a man in a blue turban who lounged just inside the gate of the compound.

"You going thieves' bazaar, your furniture finding," Nathoo told Joe calmly.

Suspicion flamed in Joe's mind. "What do you know about that?"

Nathoo shook his head. He glanced again at the man by the gate and then said in frightened tones, "Your camel, young sahib, is a strange camel."

"Do you mean he's one of those specially trained camels that can go for days without water?"

"Not that, sahib."

"Well, what then?" Joe demanded.

Just then Mr. Foster came out to call Joe. Quickly, Nathoo explained his errand. "My father shake with fever. You giving him pills, Mr. Foster?"

In spite of Joe's frown, Mr. Foster brought the medicine. Nathoo thanked him politely and left.

Usually, Joe was fond of *papoia* melon and *kunji* (cooked cereal), but this morning he was too excited to eat. He pushed back his plate and put his elbows on the table. "Dad, what do you know about that kid Nathoo?" he asked.

"He is not a Christian—yet," Mr. Foster answered.

"He's probably a thief," Joe burst out and told his father his reasons for suspecting the boy.

"He does come from a family of thieves," Mr. Foster admitted. "We'll go to thieves' bazaar as he suggests.

Probably we'll be able to buy our things back for very little. I'm sure it is the jewels they were after."

"What on earth is 'thieves' bazaar'?" Joe asked, wide-eyed.

"A place where the thieves, who really cannot use your things, sell them back cheaply. Usually they steal only as much as they need to keep alive. It's safer for them to steal small amounts rather than to take so much that the government would put them all in jail. Of course, a fortune in jewels is an unusual temptation."

On the way to the lonely spot where thieves' bazaar was held, Joe looked down at the camel and wondered about Nathoo's words. The camel was a big fine animal, and fast. He knelt; he rose; he turned at the usual signals. What had Nathoo meant?

A thin man in a blue turban who was head of the thieves' bazaar told them they could have their things. They could even have the brass jar with the cut halves of the 10-rupee notes for 10 rupees altogether.

They tied the camel outside the gate and went into a small courtyard to check their belongings. While Mr. Foster bargained with the owner of a bullock cart, Joe stared at the turbaned man. Why, he was the man Joe had seen at their gate that morning!

"I think I'll leave you here to make sure they load everything on the cart," Mr. Foster said to Joe when he had made his bargain. "I'll barely have time to make the train if I take the camel and leave now."

Joe watched his dad hurry out to the gate, then stop short. Now Joe saw what his father had seen—Lal was gone! How could the camel have disappeared so quickly?

Chapter 4

JOE RAN to his dad. "Could Lal have gotten loose by himself?" he whispered.

"Not a chance," Mr. Foster answered. "I had him tied tightly. Somebody's stolen him, Joe. I'll miss my train, and I won't be able to get the jewels to Bombay where they will be safe."

The man in the blue turban shrugged his shoulders when Mr. Foster asked him who had taken the camel. Nobody else was nearby but an old woman, frying *chapatties* (pancakes) by the roadside.

The woman could remember nothing until Mr. Foster gave her six annas. Then she suddenly recalled that a boy in a pinkish turban had ridden the camel away.

The driver of the bullock cart came to the gate and politely invited Mr. Foster to ride in the cart with his first load. When the missionary shook his head, the man jumped up to his seat between the two big white bullocks. He gave their tails a hard twist, and was off in a cloud of dust.

"Let's go right to the police and tell them Nathoo stole our camel," Joe said hotly.

But Mr. Foster said in his patient way, "We don't know that Nathoo stole the camel." He started walking swiftly along the deserted road, with Joe trudging angrily beside him. "We don't even know that it's been stolen. We'll probably get it back just as we got the furniture back. Somebody just took it away to be sure I missed my train."

"But who knew you were going to take the train?" Joe demanded. "Nobody except Nathoo, who is always listening around our house."

"Anybody who knew about the jewels could guess that I would take them to the nearest city," Mr. Foster answered. "Somehow, Joe, we've got to keep those jewels safe until tomorrow morning. I'll have to catch the train then."

"How about asking some Indian Christians to help you?"

"Anybody who knows about these jewels is in danger, Son. I'd rather handle them myself."

A wave of anger washed over Joe. "That's just like you, Dad!" he burst out. "You're always thinking about other people. If we got Nathoo put in jail now, it might scare the others."

But Mr. Foster shook his head. "Nathoo is worth more than all the jewels, Joe. I'm hoping to win him for Christ. Accusing him of a crime that I'm not sure he committed wouldn't be the way."

It seemed to Joe that the walk home would never end. Heat waves shimmered dizzily in the still air. The flat, discouraged looking land, the dusty palm trees, and the jungly patches of thorn bush made Joe long to be back in the United States.

As if his father had read Joe's thoughts, he said, "There are not many places in the world where a queen would give away her jewels to start a hospital, Joe. India is a wonderful land. Don't be discouraged so soon."

"You really like it here, don't you, Dad?"

"I don't like it; it's too hot. But I love it. You will too."

The sight of the low white mission bungalow with its red-tiled roof was so pleasant that Joe began to think his father was right. After the hot road almost any spot in the shade looked good.

They turned in the gate just as the bullock driver was leaving after delivering his last load. On the veranda was a familiar pile of things—the blue sofa, the worn armchair and desk, some rugs and pictures.

"We'll move these in when it gets a little cooler," Mr. Foster told Joe. "Better go and lie down until you feel better."

Joe didn't argue. His shoulders sagged as he started to his bedroom. But at the door he lifted his head, startled by what he saw.

The bedroom was empty. His bed, chair, table, and the chest of drawers were all gone.

Joe stepped across the hall to his parents' room. Empty too! He called to his father. "What do you think of these people now?"

His father inspected the empty rooms before answering. Then he said, "Well, they haven't dug up the compound yet. An Indian would bury his treasure. I'm hoping that's what they would expect me to do. That's why I'm carrying the jewels around."

"I suppose we'll just wait a few hours and then we can buy back our beds."

"Maybe, Joe. But in the meantime, we'll have to have some help. I'm beginning to agree with you on that point.

Go to N'rain Singh's house—it's a mile south of here on the same road. Ask him to come at once."

Joe grabbed his sun hat and was out of the door before his father could change his mind. As he ran toward the gate, the sun seemed a little less hot and the heat waves didn't make him so dizzy.

He opened the gate just in time to let in Nathoo, still wearing his huge pinkish turban.

Joe demanded what he wanted. Nathoo replied that he needed some more medicine for his father. Joe wanted to say a lot to Nathoo, but he decided that the important thing was to find N'rain Singh. Out of the corner of his eye he saw his father come out on the veranda to meet Nathoo.

Chapter 5

OUTSIDE THE GATE, Joe turned in the direction of the Christian's house. He almost tripped over a huge camel, kneeling by the hedge, contentedly munching thorns. Joe looked at the camel from several angles to make sure he was not mistaken. No doubt about it. Lal, the mystery camel, was back.

Joe put his hand to his aching head. What next?

Well, maybe at least his father could start to Bombay. Maybe he would take N'rain Singh or one of the other Christians with him on the camel. He'd go back and tell his father.

Joe made sure that Lal was securely tied to a neem tree and then went back into the compound. Mr. Foster was sitting on the veranda, with Nathoo squatting on the tiles at his feet. The missionary was telling the boy the Bible story of the lost coin.

"The coin means a person's soul, Nathoo," he was explaining. "It is of more value than all the jewels in the world, even a queen's treasure."

"Dad! The camel's back!" Joe called as he ran up the steps.

"Maybe now you can—"

"Yes. Good!" Mr. Foster said quietly. "I told you I thought he'd return. But you have an errand—remember?"

The big camel tossed his head and gave an annoyed groan at having to leave his thorny meal. But once on the road he made good time. Joe was back in a half hour with the Indian Christian.

"I will go with your father to Bombay," the man promised as they reached the compound. He added, "He is in great danger, I fear."

He hurried through the gate without waiting for Joe, who stopped to tie the camel. Suddenly Joe heard N'rain Singh's voice calling him from the veranda.

Joe dashed through the gate and ran toward the house, forgetting the camel and his weariness. In fact he forgot everything except the sight that made his heart beat heavily and his eyes mist with tears.

His father was lying by the veranda, face down. He was lying very still.

Mr. Foster groaned. He was beginning to move slightly when Joe reached him. N'rain Singh gently turned him over on his back. Then he picked up a tile which had fallen from the roof.

"Why, that must have hit Dad's head as he was going down the steps," Joe began. "But I don't see—"

He broke off, staring at something in N'rain Singh's brown hand. It was a strand of fine wire, fastened to the tile.

"Your father walked into a trap!" N'rain Singh exclaimed in a cold, angry voice. "Look, *baba* (boy), at that wire stretched across the step just above you. I noticed it and stepped over it. Your father did not. He ran into it, and the pull on the wire dislodged this tile. If he had not been wearing his pith topi, he might have been killed."

Joe bent over his father. Mr. Foster was staring around in a dazed way. "Are you all right, Dad?"

"Yes," his father answered faintly. "The jewels, Joe. See—"

Joe explored his father's pockets with shaky fingers. "The jewels are gone!" Joe exclaimed. "But I'll find them for you, Dad."

His dad managed a faint smile. "Be careful, Son. Remember, jewels are not the most important—" His voice trailed off into silence.

"We must not leave him alone again," N'rain Singh said. "There is a doctor in the next village, Joe. While you fetch him, I will guard your father."

The camel still knelt where Joe had left him, but someone had been there. Caught between the heavy saddle and the animal's hide was a note. Joe snatched it up and read aloud: *"Come with camel, young sahib."*

Nathoo must have left the message, he thought angrily. Why did Nathoo keep hinting that there was something strange about Lal?

Joe jumped on the camel's back, tugged at the cord attached to the ivory stick in the animal's nose, and started for the doctor.

But where was Nathoo now? He must have been there only a moment ago. Probably he was crouching somewhere behind a wall, waiting for Joe to walk into another trap.

Chapter 6

THE INDIAN DOCTOR was a thin young man with glasses and a kind face. He picked up his bag and came running when Joe told him Mr. Foster needed him.

He climbed onto the big saddle behind Joe, saying, "For him I will gladly come."

They were soon back at the mission compound. Joe tied Lal, then led the doctor into the bungalow. His father, conscious now, was lying on a mat. N'rain Singh was beside him. Joe said nothing about the message left on the saddle.

Mr. Foster began to tell the doctor that he had seen a strange man beckoning him from the gate. Starting out to meet him, he had been hit on the head.

While his dad was still talking, Joe wandered out to the road. Why did his father insist on trusting Nathoo? Perhaps—if Mr. Foster was right—the boy had nothing to do with the falling tile. Perhaps Joe ought to trust him too.

But how could he follow Nathoo's directions?

"Come with camel." Come where? Was he supposed to just get on Lal's back and let the big beast carry him away?

Nathoo always said that this was no ordinary camel. Why not see what would happen?

Joe loosened the tether, climbed on the camel's humped back, and gave the signal to rise. Then he let the reins hang loosely while he said softly, "Go wherever you want, Lal."

The animal set off at once at a fast trot. It seemed to know exactly where to go.

Past the adobe wall and the mud houses he trotted. He left the village behind him. Then, at a place where a jungle of dusty bushes surrounded one of the little round hills that dot the plains of India, he did a strange thing. He left the road and dropped to his knees. With Joe still on his back, he began a fast crawl across the dusty earth, zigzagging between the bushes, out of sight of the road.

Joe glanced back and saw the queer tracks the animal made—irregular lines, such as wheels or runners could not make. He had seen those tracks before—in the dust of the mission compound, after the furniture had been stolen!

"So it was you who carried the things away," Joe whispered to the camel. "No wonder no one saw you if you crawled like this. So you were specially trained. This is what Nathoo meant when he said you were different from other camels."

The camel must be taking him to the thieves' hideout, Joe decided. He had a brief sickening memory of his father lying on the ground. The thieves must have known that the blow might kill him. Was Joe going into a trap too?

But the thieves had the jewels. Why should they want Joe?

Joe's hands moved toward the reins to turn the camel aside. He still had time to return.

But something held Joe back. Maybe it was the memory of his father's faith that his prayers would be answered.

Lal was crawling straight toward a hillside now. Suddenly he dodged behind a boulder and then went into a dark opening.

Inside a cave in pitch-black darkness the camel halted. Joe sat still, afraid to move. For an instant there wasn't a sound. Then he heard movement beside him and wanted to cry out. But he bit his lip and waited silently.

After a long moment, a voice close to him whispered, "I am Nathoo, young sahib. They leaving me here with the jewels. I am tied to wall. You must loose me. Then we are going together—quickly before they come back. Your father—is he all right?"

"Yes," Joe whispered as he fumbled for his pocketknife. "His sun helmet saved him."

"That is what I hoping."

Joe could make out the walls of the vast, shadowy cave now. The boy Nathoo was a dark shadow under the pale mass of his turban. While Joe sawed at the rope that bound Nathoo, he whispered, "Aren't you afraid they'll kill you?"

"Yes," the boy whispered back. "But I am wanting to be Christ's man. Your father teaching me the way. He promise he sending me to school. Then he build hospital, making my father well." As the ropes fell away, Nathoo put a small hard bundle into Joe's hands. "The jewels," he hissed. "Hurry!"

The journey between the bushes had seemed fast before; now it was terrifyingly slow. Joe did not draw a full breath until they reached the road and turned the camel's head toward the mission bungalow. Then he asked the question that was on his mind. "Tell me, was it the man in the blue turban who planned the whole thing?"

"Yes. He my uncle. He hearing the Christians talking about the Ranee's gift for hospital. I could not stop his plans. I trying to call out the night we steal your furniture, but he striking me and making me be silent. After that I am afraid."

"And you kept trying to tell me about the camel. Father was right about you, Nathoo."

Joe turned the camel in at the mission gate. His father was sitting in a long chair on the veranda with the doctor and N'rain Singh beside him.

Joe looked at them and was thankful—and felt safe, safer than he ever had before. If God wanted them to have the money from the jewels, He would take care of Dad as he carried them to Bombay.

And Nathoo? Joe felt a new, warm respect for the boy on the camel behind him. Surely God could meet his needs too.

THE ISRAELI OIL WELL MYSTERY

Bernard Palmer

Chapter 1

RICK MacRAE let himself into the neat little house which the oil company had provided for his parents and himself in Jerash, Israel.

"Is that you, Rick?" his mother called.

"Yeah, Mom," he answered as he closed the door tightly, to shut out the burning heat.

"I'm so glad you're home." His attractive young mother, Marsha, came into the kitchen with a worried look on her face. "I pray for you all the time you're at school," she said.

"Mom, you don't need to worry about me," Rick said with some irritation. He squared his 12-year-old shoulders and stretched as tall as he could. (He was built like his dad—short and stocky.)

"Well, I heard over the radio that three Israelis were killed less than 10 miles from here last night," his mother said.

"The kids at school were talking about the murders too," Rick said, his brown eyes bright with concern. "Too bad the Arabs and Jews can't live together in peace."

Tensions in Israel had only increased since the Six-

Day War in 1967. The Arab nations had attacked Israel but she had defeated them, taking over a lot of Arab territory, including the Negev.

Now, three years later, Rick's father was supervising an oil drilling crew from the U.S. They had come at the request of the Israeli government to help find badly needed oil.

Because of fierce attacks by the Palestinian Liberation Organization (PLO), an Arab guerrilla group, Mr. Mac-Rae had set up men to guard the drilling site.

Part American Indian, Mr. MacRae was short and muscular, and as dark as any Palestinian. His face showed the strain as he came into the house that evening. "It doesn't look good, Marsha," he said as he dropped wearily into a chair and tossed his work helmet on the floor.

Mrs. MacRae, as fair as her husband was dark, leaned over and kissed her husband. "What's the matter?" she asked:

Rick looked up from his homework and grinned. Trouble might rage around them, but his parents loved each other and the Lord Jesus and that sure helped make life a lot easier.

"Somebody sawed half through a cable during the night," his father told them. "This morning it broke and dropped a drill that almost killed two men!"

He sighed and ran his fingers through his hair. "I had tripled the guard and ordered them to turn back any strangers within a quarter of a mile, but somebody still got through. He almost succeeded in ruining the well. I can't understand it."

"If I didn't trust in the Lord," Mrs. MacRae said softly, "I wouldn't be able to stand it out here at all."

Her husband took her hand and squeezed it. "I know," he answered. "I feel the way you do. If I weren't sure that the Lord sent us here, I think I'd pack up and leave before this place explodes!"

His wife looked troubled. She was silent for a long while after that.

Later, at the dinner table, Mr. MacRae turned to Rick. "Well, how'd things go at school today?"

"Oh, we kept busy," Rick said. He decided not to worry them about everything that had happened.

It hadn't been so much, really. Only he longed desperately for friends and none of the guys at school would speak to him.

When his family had left America two months before, they had looked forward to living in a new country. But Rick had trouble getting used to the school. Several different languages were spoken on the schoolgrounds, and his teachers understood most of them.

Fellows and girls were there from Germany, Russia, Italy, the United States, and a handful of other nations.

The first fellow he met was from Holland. "I can tell you're from the United States," he had said to Rick. "I'm from Holland. My name is Jacob Cohen."

"I'm Rick MacRae," Rick had said.

Jacob looked at him, then grinned, taking Rick's hand and shaking it a little awkwardly.

In class the teacher translated her instructions to the students into several languages, and the recitations were a babel of strange sounds. But the fellows all played soccer. Rick had played some back in the States and took over the position of goalie on one of the teams. He had soon learned a smattering of French, Russian, and German, enough to talk a little with those fellows. And, of course, everybody studied Hebrew.

It had been in Hebrew class one morning that it had happened. The teacher first read to them from the Book of Isaiah in Hebrew. Then students translated the same portion from that ancient Jewish language to their native tongue, whatever it happened to be.

"Now, Rick," the teacher asked after a girl had read her translation in English, "when are we to look for the Messiah?"

He had been thinking about something else. He looked up quickly, a question on his face.

"When are we to look for the coming of our Messiah?" she asked again.

"The Messiah has come," Rick responded without thinking about where he was. "Jesus Christ is the Messiah; I believe in Him as my Saviour."

A hush fell over the classroom. The teacher's face whitened.

"Any good scholar knows that our Messiah has not yet come. When he does, he will conquer our enemies and rule over us." With that rebuke his teacher changed the subject abruptly.

Throughout the rest of the morning Rick had felt sick inside. Was he the only one here who believed in Jesus as his Saviour, the true Messiah?

After school his soccer team was to have a special practice game. Rick forgot what had happened in Hebrew class until he went out onto the field. The fellows stared at him coldly as he picked up the chest protector and started to put it on.

"What are you doing with that?" Jacob asked shortly.

"We take the field first, don't we?" Rick asked.

Jacob nodded grimly. "But we've got a new goalie for this afternoon."

"Oh, OK," Rick replied easily. "What position do you want me to play?"

Jacob shook his head. "We don't need you anymore, MacRae."

"But why?" he asked. "What's the matter?"

"You're not one of us," Jacob answered.

Rick stood alone, watching numbly, while the fellows trotted out onto the field and began to play. If the guys looked at him, they stared coldly, but that was all. No one spoke.

Rick had finally turned away and scuffled home through the scorching afternoon. Some of the gang back in the States had laughed at him for talking about Christ. But they had still played with him. Here, the students seemed to hate him.

The following days were the same. Although several fellows in his sixth grade class lived close by, they would not walk to school with him. When he joined a group, the talking quieted down, and some found an excuse to leave quickly.

In class, the teacher called on him but never asked him about religion again. Rick was still glad he was a Christian, but he got more lonely and restless every day.

Chapter 2

EXACTLY A WEEK after the cable had been mysteriously cut at the well, Rick's mother came running to meet him as he walked up the hill to his home after school.

"Oh, Rick," she said excitedly. "I'm so glad you've come. There's an important transatlantic call coming in for Dad, and I can't reach him at the well."

"I'll go and get him," Rick said.

"Do be careful," she called after him.

Rick shivered a little, despite the heat. He jogged up the hill, across a field, and over another steep, rock-studded hill toward the oil well. He was glad it was daylight. The PLO rarely attacked without the protection of darkness.

He had just reached the top of the hill and was starting down the other side when he stopped short. Below him three turbaned men crouched behind rocks that bordered the trail. All had rifles.

A short distance away a Jewish boy approached, unaware of the terrible trap. Rick gasped. Now the PLO was ambushing in broad daylight, and a boy's life hung in the balance!

For an instant, Rick's heart stood still. Then he saw a big stone only a few paces ahead. It lay almost directly above the guerillas! Just the thing!

With a prayer in his heart, he darted forward, dislodged the jagged rock, and pushed it down the steep slope.

"Look out!" he shouted. "Look out!"

The rock loosened other stones and boulders and the collisions echoed through the hills. Soon the slide was a little avalanche hurtling downward.

The Arabs straightened, staring at the rocks tumbling toward them. Then with shouts of fear and surprise, they dove for safety.

The young Jew saw the avalanche and the armed men at the same instant. He leaped to one side and scrambled up a slope as the boulders thundered past.

Rick held his breath. Perhaps the outlaws would still turn back and attack. But a moment later he heard the sound of a motor and saw an old military truck careening away.

Rick was still standing there, white and shaken, when the young Israeli scrambled up beside him.

"I didn't see those Arabs until you started that avalanche," the boy burst out gratefully. "If it hadn't been for you, I don't know what would have happened."

Rick grinned happily at him. The other boy was about Rick's size. He too was dark, though his face was pale and drawn at the moment.

"I don't think I've seen you around before," Rick said.

"We just got here," the Jew said. "My dad will work on the well when he gets here."

"My dad's working on the well too. I'm Rick MacRae."

"And I'm Reuben Nordstein." They shook hands solemnly. "My father just got out of Russia. Mother and I came from America to meet him here."

Rick suddenly remembered the message he was carrying to his father. "I'm on my way to the well. Would you like to go with me?" he asked.

Together they hurried down the steep, winding path to the place where the oil rig had been set up.

Rick's father frowned thoughtfully when he heard about the transatlantic call. After a moment he turned and hurried toward the jeep.

"Come on," he called to Rick, his voice tinged with excitement. "I think I know what the call is about."

Rick turned to his new friend. "I'll see you tomorrow, Reuben."

"I'll look for you at school," agreed the boy.

Back home, Mr. MacRae took the telephone call and talked for several minutes. When he had finished, he came into the kitchen where Rick and his mother were waiting.

"I almost knew what it was," he began. "I cabled the home office for instructions last week."

"About the sabotage?" Rick's mother asked.

Mr. MacRae shook his head. "Not exactly. I guess I can tell you this in confidence. I think we've made a big oil discovery."

"You have!" his wife exclaimed. "But I thought—"

"That we are still drilling?" he finished for her. "Well, we are, but only because we think there's a bigger oil pool below the one we've hit. Our advance crews have been covering this area for the past two years, and we've found just what they predicted. This may be the biggest field in this area."

"That's great, Dad!" Rick exclaimed.

"That's why we've been so worried about sabotage. The Arabs are afraid that if we begin to draw oil up here, we'll drain one of their richest oil supplies."

Rick's eyes almost popped with excitement. "Wow!" he breathed. "Is that possible?"

"I think there's enough oil here for everyone," Dad answered.

"But what was the phone call about?" his mother prompted.

"The company wants a complete, firsthand report on the situation here," he said. "They insist that I fly to New York for a meeting."

"But, Dear! You can't leave Rick and me alone!" Mrs. MacRae cried.

"Ben Silverman is coming from Tel Aviv tomorrow to take charge of the drilling while I'm gone," he reassured them. "We've got some temporary buildings out at the well site. I thought we'd move you and Rick out there near the crew for the few days I'll be gone."

"That will be all right," she told him confidently. "I should remember that we have the Lord to look after us."

That night while Mrs. MacRae was packing, Rick's dad spoke to him seriously. "Keep your eyes open at the well. If you see anybody around who looks as though he doesn't belong there, get hold of Mr. Silverman quickly!"

"I understand," Rick answered solemnly. The danger made him tremble a bit, though he knew the Lord would help him.

Chapter 3

THE NEXT AFTERNOON Rick moved with his mother out to a cabin not far from the noisy oil rig. The following morning his dad flew out to Tel Aviv where he was to catch a plane for London and the United States. Ben Silverman had arrived at Jerash only three hours earlier to take over until Mr. MacRae returned.

When Rick and his mother got back from the airport, Reuben Nordstein was waiting to walk the two miles over the hills to school with him.

Reuben and his mother had moved out near the oil drilling site, not far from the cabin Rick and his mother were in. This was Reuben's first day in the Jerash school.

"What are the fellows like?" he asked as they walked along.

"Oh, they're OK," Rick replied. They *had* been fine until they learned that he was a Christian.

When they got to school, Reuben was taken to a different homeroom and given different classes. Rick didn't get to talk with him again until school was out that afternoon.

"Did you like it, Reuben?" he asked his friend.

"All right for the first time," Reuben replied.

Rick glanced at him quickly. Had he heard about Rick? They walked out of town and up the first rock-strewn hill without speaking.

Finally Reuben turned to him. "Rick," he said abruptly. "Why don't the fellows at school like you?"

A chill seized Rick's heart, and for a moment he did not answer. "I—" he began. "It's this way," he said, praying for the right words. "The rest of the fellows and girls in school are Jewish."

"Not all of them," Reuben declared. "Four or five American and British kids mix in with the others."

"I did too," explained Rick, "until the kids found out that I believe in Jesus Christ as the Messiah and my Saviour. Now they won't have anything to do with me."

"I see." Reuben's voice sounded distant and undecided, as if he didn't know how friendly he should be.

Rick looked at him earnestly. "I want to be friends with you, Reuben."

The Jewish boy turned and faced Rick. He searched Rick's eyes for a long moment and then answered deliberately, "I want to be friends with you too, Rick."

The boys walked along the hot, dusty road with new understanding. When they neared the oil well, they saw that something was wrong. Men were standing in excited groups, and the town doctor was running toward the machinery.

"Something's wrong!" Rick cried. They ran to the nearest group and Rick demanded, "What's the matter? What happened?"

The man looked at him blankly and Rick realized that he probably couldn't speak English.

The two boys ran up to the oil well. "What happened?"

Rick asked one of the few Americans on the job.

"It's Ben Silverman!" the American exclaimed. "I'm afraid he's hurt bad!"

"Come on!" Rick yelled to Reuben. "Let's see how bad he is!" They pushed through the tense group surrounding the injured superintendent. Mr. Silverman was lying on the ground, his face drawn with pain. One leg was doubled under him and his shoulder was bleeding badly. The doctor was bent over him, working to stop the bleeding.

"How did it happen?" Rick asked the man who was standing next to him.

"They were putting in a new section of casing," the worker said. "It slipped and struck him."

"Slipped nothing!" somebody rasped. "That was no accident, if you ask me."

"That's what I say," another put in. "Somebody was after him."

"You're not going to catch me working on this hole anymore," still another said darkly. "Two bad accidents in a week. I may be the next one!"

Rick glanced up at the speaker. He was a big leathery-skinned man with piercing black eyes and a twist to his mouth.

"No, sir," he repeated. "You're not going to catch me on this job anymore. I'm going over for my pay and get out of here before something happens to me."

Just then an ambulance skidded to a stop before the rig, and four or five men moved the injured superintendent onto a stretcher and into the waiting vehicle. Rick touched the doctor on the arm as he stepped into the ambulance.

"Is he going to be all right?" Rick asked.

The doctor turned and said, "He's painfully hurt, but he'll pull through. He won't be moving around for a while though."

Rick looked hopelessly at Reuben. But his friend was watching someone else. Rick turned and saw the worker who had said he was going to quit, moving from one group of workers to another. Instead of going to the paymaster, he was talking excitedly and waving his arms.

"I believe he's trying to talk those men into quitting too!" Reuben said. While they watched, two men laid down their tools and started walking toward the time-keeper's shed.

"You're right," Rick agreed. "Now that he's got that bunch all stirred up he's going to some more. I think he's trying to stop the drilling!" He dare not tell Reuben that his dad knew there was oil in the well—maybe the biggest oil pool the company had ever found.

Presently, the assistant superintendent, Aaron Messick, came striding out to the job and took over. He began shouting orders, but it was too late to restore order Over half the day shift drew their pay and quit.

"We'll shut down tonight," Messick stormed. "I'll put the night crew on days until we can hire enough new men to work two shifts."

"I don't like that," Rick said quietly to his companion. "Dad always works night and day, even when he's short-handed."

The boys walked past the oil rig, the big stack of pipe, or casing as the oil drillers called it, and past the time-keeper's shack. Two men were standing there talking in a language Rick didn't recognize.

Reuben clutched Rick's arm tightly and started to walk rapidly away.

"What's the matter?" Rick asked.

Reuben didn't reply until they had put considerable distance between themselves and the timekeeper's shack. Then he stopped and turned to Rick.

"That man," he said tensely, "the one with his back to us—I just heard him say something in Russian."

"What was it?" Rick asked.

"He said that 'everything is set—tonight's the night.'"

A chill danced up Rick's spine, and his heart skipped a beat. He turned slightly to look at the man Reuben had overheard and he gasped. It was the man who had talked the others into quitting! So the Russians were in on this too!

"What will we do?" Reuben said urgently.

Rick stood immovable. What could they do? His dad had told him to let Ben Silverman know if he saw or heard anything suspicious. But Ben was hurt and in the hospital.

"We'd better go to the assistant superintendent," Rick said. "Someone has to do something."

They went over to his dad's office which Aaron Messick was using temporarily. Just as they got there, Messick came striding out and jumped into the jeep.

"Mr. Messick!" Rick shouted to him. "Mr. Messick! I've got something to tell you!"

The assistant superintendent started the motor with a roar and swung the car into the road. In a few moments, it was hidden in a billow of dust.

"He's going home," an aide said shortly. "He won't be back until morning."

The two boys walked slowly away from the building.

"There isn't anyone else we can trust," Rick half whispered when they were alone. "We'll just have to keep our eyes open and do what we can."

Chapter 4

REUBEN GOT PERMISSION to stay with Rick that night and shortly after 9 o'clock they went into the little bedroom to bed.

"Mother would never allow us to sit out by the rig," Rick whispered, "but we can see what's going on from here."

The boys knelt on the floor in the dark room, looking intently out the little window at the oil rig. It was dark now, but the moon was shining brilliantly and the gaunt, ugly structure was bathed in light.

Half an hour passed, then an hour. All was quiet at the rig. Aaron Messick had kept the guard at the same strength around the well site. But since the rig was shut down for the night he did not post guards at the well itself.

"We're lucky the moon's so bright," Reuben said. "We can see anything that moves within a hundred yards of the well."

Rick nodded.

Their legs stiffened, and Rick's arm went to sleep. He started to rub it briskly.

"You know," the Israeli boy said, "you told me how the

kids at school left you alone after you told them you were a Christian?"

Rick nodded.

"Why did you tell them, anyway? Why didn't you just keep quiet about it? Then everything would have been all right."

"I couldn't do that," Rick replied. "Jesus died on the cross so I could be saved. I love Him and want others to love Him too."

Reuben sat quiet for a long while. "That sounds something like the radio program my parents and I used to listen to in Russia," he said. "It was from a station in Europe."

"Hey, maybe that was Trans World Radio!" Rick said eagerly.

"That's it," Reuben replied. "We used to draw the blinds and lock the doors and turn the radio down real low. The man talked about Jesus and how He died on the cross for us. But you know, Jews don't believe in Jesus. He was born in a manger and then died a poor man. We expect the Messiah to come and conquer our enemies and then be our King."

"But Jesus came and . . ."

A slight noise outside choked the words in Rick's throat. They both heard it and sprang to the window. Clouds had come up while they were talking, clouds that shrouded the rig in darkness.

"Listen!" Rick exclaimed under his breath.

This time the noise was unmistakable. Someone was out at the derrick. Someone who had no business being there!

Rick and Reuben leaned against the window frame, listening breathlessly. Ages seemed to pass. Then they heard it again—a muffled metallic ring, as if someone did not want to be heard.

"Did you hear that?" Reuben whispered. "Somebody's out there!"

Rick nodded. His heart hammered furiously and his hands trembled.

"Wh-what are we going to do?" his Israeli friend stammered.

Rick didn't know. His dad was gone, and he didn't know anyone else he could trust. The sound was repeated louder and sharper, as if someone were anxious to finish the job and get away.

"Maybe you should call your mom," Reuben suggested.

"Or maybe we can just scare away whoever is out there," Rick said. "Wanta try?"

"Well—OK," Reuben said slowly.

With a prayer on his lips, Rick tiptoed past his mother's bedroom and out into the hush of the shadowy night. Reuben was right behind him.

They walked quietly forward, past the darkened time-keeper's shack and the office of the superintendent. Just beyond lay the big generators, the pipe, and then the derrick.

Whoever was there could be sawing a cable or weakening the winch, or doing one of a hundred things that could cause the drilling to break down. He moved faster. Time meant everything now.

At the big pile of steel pipe, Rick stopped so quickly that Reuben bumped into him. The oil rig was some 25 or 30 yards beyond. Rick could make out the towering hulk of the derrick and the vague outline of the machinery that rose within it. He tried to identify every dark shape to determine whether anything was there that did not belong.

He had seen the well a thousand times. Yet when it came to remembering just how things were—he stiffened. Something moved on the platform inside the derrick! Reuben saw it too. He grasped Rick's arm and squeezed hard.

Rick could just make out the shape of a man crouching on the platform. Rick knew he didn't belong there, but what could two boys do against a desperate man? A light flickered like the flame of a match! That could well mean only one thing—dynamite!

Rick looked around, his thoughts racing wildly. Then he noticed the long pipes and thrust his head into the end of one. "Hey, you!" he bellowed. "Get out of there!" His voice rumbled and roared through the long pipe. Reuben, standing beside him, jumped as though he had been struck.

The figure on the derrick straightened and froze. Silently, he whirled and leaped off the platform. In a moment he was lost in the night.

"Wowie!" Reuben managed. "You really scared him away."

Rick laughed shakily. "Let's go and take a look at that derrick!"

As they stumbled toward the looming machine, the moon suddenly peeked past a cloud, bathing the scene in bright light.

"He was standing just about there," the Israeli boy said, pointing to the platform.

Clambering up, Rick scanned the platform. "Look at this!" he exclaimed.

"What is it?" Reuben asked. "It looks like a piece of white cord."

"I think it's a fuse," Rick said.

"That means dynamite!" the Jewish lad exclaimed.

Rick quickly followed the fuse to the charge of TNT. "Look at that!" he said. Enough to blow everything here to bits!"

Carefully he picked it up and carried it back to the house.

"What'll we do with it?" Reuben asked, staring at it dubiously.

"Put it under our bed until morning," Rick replied.

"Not under the bed *I'm* sleeping on!" Reuben said. "I'm heading for home!"

"Look, as long as we keep it away from fire, it's safe to handle," Rick said.

Chapter 5

THE NEXT morning before school, the boys told Mrs. MacRae what had happened.

"Next time you two let me know when you think there's trouble and I'll call the authorities. You could have been killed," she said.

"But, Mom, it all happened too fast," Rick said.

"You should have told me you suspected trouble," she reminded him. "Now be careful with that dynamite. Imagine, bringing it into the house!" She put her hand on her forehead and groaned.

After eating, the boys took the dynamite over to the assistant superintendent, Aaron Messick, and told him what had happened. He sat at his desk, scowling through their story as he fingered the end of the fuse.

"This is serious," he said at last. "This is very serious. We'll have to check into it right away. Why, everything could have been ruined here if you hadn't discovered it."

He followed them to the door and thanked them for their help. "But if I were you boys," he concluded, "I'd stay away from that derrick at night. It might be verv dangerous there!"

Neither Rick nor Reuben spoke until they had passed the guard. Then Reuben turned to his friend. "Did you get the feeling I did that Mr. Messick wasn't very excited?"

Rick nodded. "And when he told us to stay away from the derrick, it sounded almost like a threat. I wonder about him."

That afternoon, as soon as the last class was out at school, the two boys met and started home.

"Some of the fellows were talking to me this noon, Rick," Reuben said as they hurried along. "They wondered why we're friends."

Rick looked at him quickly, his heart skipping. "What did you say?"

"I told them you might be a Christian, but you're still a nice guy," Reuben said, grinning.

"Thanks," Rick said. "I sure wish you knew the Lord Jesus as your Saviour too."

"But I'm a Jew," Reuben said. "I'm one of God's chosen people. I don't need a Saviour."

Rick was quiet a minute, then he answered. "Reuben, the Bible tells us that everyone needs a Saviour. Your prophet, Isaiah, said that we all, like sheep, have gone astray. That means we all need a Saviour from sin if we're going to live in heaven with God."

Reuben was silent for several minutes. "I didn't know those things were in our Scriptures," he said finally. "As soon as my dad gets here, I'd like to have you talk to him."

By this time they had reached the oil well site. The guard checked them at the entrance, and they noticed twice as many were posted around the property as in the morning. Two guards stood alertly beside the derrick.

"It looks like Mr. Messick believed us after all," Reuben said.

The crew quit work at 5 o'clock, and new guards came to patrol the area. Rick and Reuben passed the new guards as they went to the little shack where the Israeli boy had lived since his father had been assigned to the crew.

"Did you see those guards?" Rick whispered excitedly. "One of them did all the talking about quitting yesterday. And the other is the fellow who was with him."

Reuben nodded slowly, his eyes big.

Just then Aaron Messick came out of the superintendent's office, got into the jeep, and drove away.

"Did you notice how he looked at that guard?" Reuben asked. "Neither one spoke, but it was almost as though he passed on a message with his eyes."

"I'd give a lot to know whether he goes into town or somewhere else," Rick observed. "I never saw him take that briefcase with him before."

"Why don't we climb up that hill?" Reuben said. "Maybe we can see which way he goes."

By the time they had climbed to the top of the hill, Messick's jeep had disappeared.

"Where do you suppose he went?" Rick asked. "He couldn't have gotten to town so soon. And there aren't any roads that turn off, unless he went out across country. I don't know why he'd do that."

A low voice spoke behind them. The boys straightened suddenly. Rick turned cautiously about. A dark, turbaned Arab, dressed in khaki, stood there with a long rifle in his hand. The PLO!

He spoke again. Rick didn't know what he said, but he

understood the menacing motion the man made with his rifle as he directed them down the steep, rocky slope.

"W-w-what should we do?" Reuben stammered.

Rick gulped. "Follow him, I guess."

"But I—I'm a Jew," Reuben protested, his eyes full of fear.

"And I look like one," Rick said grimly.

"He'll probably shoot me!" Reuben said.

"We'll have to trust the Lord . . . ," Rick's words were cut short as the impatient Arab guerrilla shoved the rifle into Rick's back.

Chapter 6

THE BOYS stumbled down the steep slope ahead of the growling Arab, skirted another hill, and came upon an Arabian horse tied to a bush. Ahead, almost hidden by a large stone, was Messick's American Oil Company jeep.

Rick started at the sight of the jeep and almost cried out. Reuben saw it too and elbowed him as the Arab stopped them and motioned them to remain where they were.

"We've got to get out of here!" Rick whispered. "If the Arabs don't finish us off, I wouldn't be surprised if that traitor Messick would. "

Seconds later an opportunity came. Their Arab captor stepped forward to call out to his companions. Silently Rick grasped Reuben's arm and pulled him back around a boulder. Crouching and running on their toes, they darted from the protection of one stone to another, gradually advancing up the slope. All of a sudden a shout from below was followed by a volley of shots that smacked into the stones and ground around them. Then they heard a mad babble of voices.

"Come on!" Rick urged. "We've got to get higher."

A thick, guttural voice broke in above the others and instantly all was quiet. Rick and Reuben hugged a boulder and waited breathlessly.

"That man is talking in Russian," the Israeli boy informed Rick. "He's saying, 'Did the boys see our guest? That is the important thing!'"

The Arab who had captured them spoke excitedly to the others, then a voice answered in Russian and Reuben translated: "'There wasn't a chance. They were only here a moment.'"

"Let them go," the Russian ordered. "We have more important business to tend to. But keep a sharp watch and if you see them, shoot! We can't let anything spoil things now!"

The boys waited for any further sound from below. They could catch only snatches of quiet conversation. Fifteen tense minutes passed, then Rick whispered, "You know, Reuben, those guys don't suspect that we're still around here. I've got an idea!"

"I think the best idea is to get away as fast as we can," the young Israeli said.

"If we could slip down close enough to hear what they're saying," proposed Rick, "maybe we could find out the answers to a lot of questions."

"You're not serious, are you, Rick?"

"Sure I am. They won't be watching for us. They think we're back home, shaking in our boots."

"Well, they're half right," said Reuben, trying to smile.

Rick closed his eyes and prayed quietly for guidance and safety. Then he said, "I think we'd better sneak down there and see what we can find out."

Carefully, they crept down, moving from one huge,

protective boulder to the next. They could hear the low murmur of voices, but could make out nothing that was said.

"I wonder if Messick is really there," Reuben whispered when they stopped to rest.

"That's one of the things we've got to find out," Rick said.

"That jeep sure looked like his," Reuben added. "I don't think there's another like it around here."

Rick inched forward again. Soon he could hear the men clearly. This time he recognized Messick's voice, talking in rapid English.

"But I've got to have more money," he was saying. "With all the risks I'm taking I've got to get a bigger cut."

"You'll have more money," the Russian retorted, also in English, "when you carry this off successfully. If things had gone as we planned, you could have collected today. You know as well as I do that the delay gives our *friends* time to stop us."

"Everything was set for last night," Messick snarled. "If it hadn't been for those nosy kids, we wouldn't have had a mix-up."

The Russian spoke again. Reuben translated softly in Rick's ear. "I should have had the Arabs finish them off. They'd have done it gladly enough." The boys pressed forward intently as they heard someone open the lock on a case and swing back the lid.

"Here it is," the Russian said. "Be extra careful of it and use it quickly."

"Are you sure that's enough?" Messick asked. "It doesn't look like much."

"There's enough nitro in that bottle to blow up the well

three times. Just be extra careful of it or you won't be around to collect any money."

"Don't worry," Messick answered. "I'll take care of it."

"Be sure and get it in the right place," the Russian was saying, "and use it before MacRae gets back."

They had heard enough . . . almost too much to bear. White-faced, Rick turned to signal Reuben. He thought he was standing solidly, but he jarred a loose stone that slid down, down, and banged sharply on the hood of the jeep.

"Someone's up there!" shouted Messick in alarm.

The Russian spoke sharply and stormed up the hill while the Arabs threw their rifles to their shoulders and searched the boulder-strewn slope with keen eyes.

They had no chance to run! No time even to move. The Russian clambered up the slope directly above the jeep. He spoke furiously as he spied their shrinking figures.

The boys were speechless with fear as he pointed a gun and motioned for them to come out. They stumbled to their feet and staggered down to the jeep.

Messick appeared as frightened as the boys when he recognized Rick. His face was pasty and the sweat stood out on his forehead. "What should we do?" he whined. "I didn't want to get involved in murder!"

The Russian barked something in his own language as Messick picked up the case and ran for the jeep.

Reuben took advantage of the Russian's excited direction to Messick to translate in a whisper to Rick: "He's told Messick to get back to the well and plant that nitro—that time is running out. He says he's turning us over to Zaid Pasha. He's a leader in the PLO!"

Rick shivered as the Russian turned back to them and

laughed cruelly. He would stop at nothing to accomplish his evil purposes.

Sweat beaded Rick's forehead and the palms of his hands. His lower lip quivered. He looked quickly at Reuben and saw that the Israeli boy had bowed his head and was moving his lips silently. Was he praying?

Chapter 7

THE RUSSIAN leader snarled an order to the Arabs, indicating the two boys with his hand.

The Arabs jabbed the boys with rifle ends and they started off, talking among themselves.

The boys understood the language just enough to pick out a few words. "Tomorrow we'll take them to Pasha. In the meantime, we will put them in the Cave of El-Hamman."

An Arab grabbed Reuben roughly by the arm and jerked him about. "Come on, you Jewish brat." He spoke in English. "We can't waste the night on you." He pushed Reuben especially unmercifully over the steep rocky trail ahead of him.

"Are you OK?" Rick spoke in a half-whisper to his companion, as the guerrilla let him slow down.

"So far," Reuben replied.

It was getting dark. The sun had dropped behind the horizon. Long shadows were giving way to the blackness of night as they walked up the steep hill. Finally they reached the Cave of El-Hamman, and the Arabs prodded Rick and Reuben inside.

The others waited outside while the one who spoke English took charge of them.

He ordered Reuben to tie up Rick first with a rope, then he turned to Reuben and promised, "I'll tie you so tight you'll never get loose!" He jerked Reuben's hands behind his back and pulled his feet back to them.

"My mother and father were killed by Jews," he grated as he yanked savagely on the rope. "Tonight I'll be back to get my revenge!"

He didn't forget to check and tighten the knots Reuben had tied. Then with a satisfied look, he turned and hurried out of the cave.

"Boy, I was scared he was going to shoot you right away," Rick said.

Reuben nodded, fear making his eyes large.

"Would you mind if I prayed?" Rick asked. "Only God can help us now." He closed his eyes and talked to God about their need, asking for special protection for Reuben.

When he opened his eyes, he noticed Reuben's face was red and he turned aside so Rick could not see he'd been crying.

Rick's thoughts turned to Messick. He ought to be getting back to the oil well by this time. Maybe he had already planted that bottle of nitroglycerine where it would smash the well and everything near it to bits. He trembled as he suddenly realized that his mother would be in the house within 100 yards of the derrick!

Grimly he began to wiggle his hands. He was tied tightly in a sitting position so he managed to scoot and slide over to where Reuben was lying on his stomach. "Try loosening these knots with your teeth, Reuben," he directed.

Reuben had a difficult time rolling on his side and finding the knots with his teeth. While he worked, Rick prayed earnestly, desperately.

"Are you getting anywhere?" Rick asked at last.

"I don't know," came the muffled reply. "It seems to be loosening a little, but I can't quite get it . . . There!" he exclaimed excitedly. "I've got one knot loose. There are two or three others, but I don't think they're quite as tight."

"O God," Rick prayed aloud. "Help Reuben get my hands loose. Just help him to get the knots untied and help us to get back to the oil well before . . ."

As Rick finished praying, the Israeli boy freed Rick's hands. Quickly Rick loosened his feet and went to work on the knots that bound Reuben. Moments later they were both free.

They hurried outside the cave. "We've got to get back to the well as fast as we can!" Rick said. But outside the cave he stopped uncertainly. "Do you remember which way we came?" he asked.

"I was over here once before on a hike," Reuben said. "We aren't too far from the well."

"You lead the way," Rick urged.

"We've got to be careful not to make any more noise than we have to," Reuben whispered. "I can't tell where those Arabs are in the dark."

Rick looked back to see three shadowy figures making their way up the slope to the cave.

"They're coming back to the cave after us!" he exclaimed. "Come on! If they catch us this time, it'll be the end!"

The boys started to run, scrambling up over the rocks

to the crest of the hill and sliding down the other side.

"Do you think they saw us?" Reuben whispered.

"Let's not wait to see," Rick answered hoarsely.

Somehow they managed to get down that slope, across the little valley, and up the next hill. Below them stood the oil derrick, its shape faint in the moonlight.

"Everything's still all right!" Rick gasped.

"But we must warn our mothers so they can get out of the explosion area," Reuben said.

"Ok, you go get them. I'll get the guard."

Reuben turned toward the houses and Rick hurried down the hill toward the derrick.

The guard at the entrance stopped him. But when he recognized the son of the boss, he waved him on. Rick hesitated. He didn't know whom he could trust, but he decided to take a chance. "I need help!" he called.

The guard hurried over and Rick whispered a brief explanation of what was going on. Rick wasn't sure the man was convinced.

"We don't have much time," Rick urged him.

"OK, you wait here while I check the derrick," the guard said. He was about to climb the platform, when the door to the superintendent's office opened. Out came Messick his arms loaded with boxes. He stopped suddenly when he saw Rick; then he ran for the jeep. Rick ran after him with the guard close behind.

"Stop! Where did you put that bottle?" Rick shouted.

Caught, Messick tried to bluff his way out. "What do you mean, boy? You're crazy. Don't bother me with your fantasies." He started to step into the jeep.

A sudden inspiration struck Rick. He sprinted over to the switches that started the machinery and called out,

"I think I'll just start this thing and see what happens!"

"Wait!" Messick yelled. "You'll blow us all to bits!"

At that the guard aimed his rifle at Messick and ordered him into the timekeeper's shack for safekeeping. Rick phoned the authorities and within minutes a large group of Israeli soldiers bounced in by truck. Some hunted for the nitroglycerin while others fanned out into the hills to round up the terrorists.

They turned on bright floodlights and soon found the nitro. It was suspended on a thin, strong cord 150 feet into the well. The cord was tied in such a way that the instant the machinery was started the bottle would be slammed against the steel casing, destroying the whole project.

After hearing that a cablegram had been sent to his father, Rick hurried away to find his mother. A soldier directed him to a hillside. Rick stumbled through the night till he found Reuben and Mrs. Nordstein huddled together with his mother.

Mrs. MacRae cried for joy and hugged Rick. "Now we know what it really means to 'Trust in the Lord with all thine heart . . . and He shall direct thy paths,'" she said thankfully.

"Rick," said Reuben quietly, "I think I'm beginning to understand that Jesus really is God's Son, the Messiah. I told Mother how He answered your prayers—and mine. She said she trusted in Jesus Christ long ago when she heard those radio broadcasts in Russia. But she was afraid to tell Dad and me. Now we're going to tell him together when he gets here from Haifa."

Rick looked closely at Mrs. Nordstein. Even in the dim light, he could see that her happiness was real. God was working a miracle of new life in this Jewish family.

"I can't wait to tell Dad everything," Rick said to his mother as they started toward their cabins. "So much has happened!"

"He'll be very proud of his detective son," Mrs. MacRae said, smiling.

Rick just grinned and leaped over a boulder. His heart was full of thanksgiving.